MASKED & MISERABLE

A SACRED HEARTS MC NOVELLA (BOOK 3.5)

A.J. DOWNEY

COPYRIGHT

ISBN: 978-0692367131

Edited by Barbara J. Bailey

Book design by Maggie Kern

Cover art by Dar Albert at Wicked Smart Designs

Dedication

To Jacqueline Denn & Lia Rees, for trying to cut me out of the snarl of formatting issues in order to get this series and all my other works into paperback in addition to the e-reader format. Thanks for liking my work enough to want to share it with more people, and thank you even more for having a generous spirit to help me out. Squick's story may be small but it has a lot of heartfelt sentiments to it, like I do for all your help and support. And to all my enterprising heterosexual male friends who read this for me. Some of you couldn't get past the sex scenes without blushing, laughing, and getting real uncomfortable, and some of you couldn't get past the sex scenes, period, but you all tried and you all gave me the feedback I needed. Thank you all for being open-minded enough to give it a real shot. I know it wasn't your thing, but you did it anyway, because you love me. I love you too.

1

S quick...

"Andy, do you have time for a late consult?" I looked up from my inventory and squinted at Ashton. It was close to closing time.

"Yeah! Yeah. Hold on just a sec." I hurriedly put things away in my tool drawers and stood up. I followed Ashton out into the lobby area and blinked in astonishment.

Holy shit.

"Hi."

He was fucking... Holy shit!

"Squick, are you okay?" Ashton's voice snapped me out of it.

"Yeah! Hi, what're you looking at having done, man?" I stuffed my hands in my pockets and rocked back and forth in my worn black All-Stars.

He was amazing. Exquisite. Just... wow. He was shorter than me by a head, but that's not surprising. I'm like six-foot-five, which made him like five-nine or so. He was slender in that way... that just... shit... just turned me the fuck on. I didn't like guys that were overly built-out. He had that willowy look to him, muscular, sure but more of a whipcord-over-bone kind. His hair was black, except for the front, where it was on fire. Either he, or someone he knew had helped him, dye the front shock of his hair in reds, oranges, yellows, and even whites so it looked like a fireburst in front, over his brow. The locks of hair brushed his pale forehead and I wanted to reach out and smooth them away.

He had these liquid, deep-brown eyes behind a pair of wire-rimmed oval glasses that fit his face, making him more handsome, not less. His hands were stuffed into comfortably worn light jeans. I couldn't see much skin. He had on a thin, long-sleeved, army-green v-neck sweater, a white crewneck tee peeking out at the throat. The jeans were scrunched over a pair of black Doc Marten shoes and the backs of 'em were frayed from too long stepping on them.

This guy was my kind of hot and my mouth was suddenly dry just looking at him. I realized I hadn't been listening to a damned word he'd said so far, and so I quickly tuned in.

"I'm a musician," he was saying. He pulled his hands out of his pockets and pushed back the sleeves on his sweater to his elbows and I was mesmerized by his hands, large with long fingers.

"Okay," I said.

"I wanted a line of music from here to here." He held up his arm and indicated from his wrist to his elbow on the outside blade of his forearm. He was fucking phenomenal! Whipcord over bone, just as I'd suspected. I followed the delicate tracery of his veins which stood out on the backs of his hands.

I nodded.

"Should be doable. You have any other ink?" He blushed and his kissable lips pulled into a smile.

"No, this would be my first," he said.

"No problem, man. So, you said you were a musician, was there a specific line of music you wanted? Were you thinking just some random notes or did you want something like sheet music, lines and all?"

His smile broadened.

"Actually..." He dug a piece of folded paper out of his wallet and handed it to me. I unfolded it and found a perfect line of music across the page.

I held it up landscape style and said,

"C'mere, let me see."

He came forward and held up his arm. I held the paper against it and went into work mode. I sucked my teeth and contemplated.

"Gimme, like, five minutes?" I asked. Ashton beamed at me and returned to her spot at the front counter.

"Sure!" he said and brightened.

"What's your name?" I asked.

"Aaron." Aaron... wow. Even his name was hot.

"Hey, Aaron, I'm Andy; most people around here just call me Squick." I stuck out my hand. *Touch me, yes, please touch me.*

Aaron shook my hand and smiled. "Nice to meet you, Andy."

I felt my cock twitch in my jeans just at the sound of my name on his lips. I let his hand go abruptly. It had been warm, his skin soft, his fingertips calloused. Holy shit. This was bad. Like *really* bad.

"Be right back, Aaron." I put on my best smile as I said it and I went for the Thermofax to see about making a stencil, sure, but more to calm my shit. It'd been a while since I'd had such a visceral reaction to someone. Aaron was fucking attractive as hell! I cringed, leaning on the table that supported the machine and took a deep breath. I couldn't do this, I couldn't let Trig see...

"Andy?" I turned and looked at Ashton.

Fuck. That obvious? I wondered.

She shut the door behind her and sighed out.

"You okay?" she asked, her sunlit eyes clouded with concern.

"Yeah, just needed a sec to make a stencil." I feigned innocence.

She smiled gently.

"You need to stop hiding," she murmured, "It's tearing you up inside." She hugged me and for a second, I was too stunned to hug her back. Then I wrapped my long arms around her narrow shoulders and back and smiled, acutely aware of the touch of sadness it held.

"I'm fine," I said and felt queasy at the lie. She smiled up at me a little sadly and nodded after carefully considering my face. The woman read me like a book.

"Okay. See you later then, Ethan and I are heading home." She let me have the lie for now, didn't push, and I smiled again, with a little less sadness and a whole lot more guilt.

"Okay, I'll close up after I'm finished with Aaron," I promised. She nodded and slipped out, shutting the door behind her. Coward that I am, I gave myself two or three more minutes before heading out. Trig and Ashton were at the door to the shop. He pulled the cord on the 'Open' sign and it winked out.

"Night, Bro. See you tomorrow," he said, and I nodded.

"Night, Trig," I called out, waving absently and with one last lingering look from Ashton, they left. It was just me and Aaron. Zander and the rest of the guys had left an hour or more ago, thank fuck. I felt the tension in my neck and shoulders ease marginally.

"Ashton get your ID and have you fill out the paperwork?" I asked.

"Yeah, yeah! Right here." He handed me his stuff as he spoke.

"Cool, great, come on back." I led him back to my station and motioned for him to have a seat.

"Can you take off the sweater?" I asked and swallowed hard. He smiled and pulled the long-sleeved shirt over his head. My breath caught when the tee underneath rode up over his stomach, flat with a light dusting of dark hair, a happy trail leading down into his pants. Jesus H. Christ... I wanted to lick him.

"Hold your arm out like this," I showed him what I needed and he complied. I held up the stencil and nodded before setting to work. I sprayed down the area with green hospital soap, holding a handful of paper towels underneath to keep from dripping all over his lap. Aaron was smiling, his liquid deep-brown eyes watching me from behind his sexy-as-hell lenses.

"How long have you been doing this?" he asked.

"Going on six years now. Started my apprenticeship early, about sixteen, with the drawing and the cleaning and the general scut-work." I used a safety razor to shave the light dusting of hair from the area, more precautionary than anything.

"Yeah? I thought you had to be eighteen to even set foot in one of these places," he mused.

"You do. I lied my ass off. Had my first tattoo done when I was sixteen too." I smiled and lifted my pant leg, pointing to a black-and-white cartoon comic book guy, Johnny the Homicidal Maniac, on the inside of my right leg midway between ankle and knee.

"Is that Johnen Vasquez?" he exclaimed and I startled. Most people knew Invader Zim, not a whole lot of folks knew Johnny the Homicidal Maniac or Squee, and even less knew who the hell Johnen Vasquez was, let alone that he was the creator of the characters.

"Yeah," I said and eyed Aaron speculatively.

"I love Nny and Squee!" he exclaimed. I carefully laid the stencil along his arm but I was shaking some and it folded in on itself. I sniffed, washed off his arm and tried again – and failed again. The damned lines weren't straight, the treble clef higher at the elbow than the notes at the end towards his wrist.

"I have Nailbunny and the Doughboys on me too," I said, and tried the stencil for a third time.

"That's awesome!" he laughed and his eyes danced with happy. I suppressed a groan and hung my head. God damn. Failed the stencil again.

"Problem?" he asked concerned.

"Just having a tough time getting it straight. Stencil is the most important part of the tat." I licked my lips. Wait, did he just follow that a little too closely?

"Yeah, no, I get it," he said startled. We were silent and finally I got the damned thing on straight. I held up a hand mirror.

"Good?" I asked.

He inspected it in the glass and nodded slowly after a minute.

"Yeah, good," he declared, all smiles.

"Okay, cool." I got one of my liner needles installed on my very favorite gun and tapped the pedal experimentally. Aaron jumped slightly at the loud buzz of the gun.

"Does it hurt much?" he asked dubiously, and I smiled.

"Ever do any stupid shit when you were a kid?" I asked. He smiled a one-sided smile, and I think my fucking heart stopped.

"Didn't we all?" he asked. I grinned.

"Fair point," I conceded. "Okay, more specifically, did you ever stick a nine-volt battery on your tongue?" His eyes widened and he blushed the hottest shade of pink. I laughed and he cracked a grin.

"Yeah," he said finally, laughing with me.

"Feels pretty much exactly like that," I told him. He leaned back and huffed out a relieved breath.

"Okay, that sucked, but it didn't suck too bad." He was still and thoughtful for a second then he nodded, having apparently psyched himself up enough to go through with it.

"You ready?" I asked anyway, and he gave a curt nod.

"Ready," he affirmed, and so I dipped the needle, smeared some A&D over where I was starting and dug in. He hissed out a breath that carried with it the scent of spearmint and I smiled, laying in one long line, where the notes were gonna rest. I let up.

"Not too bad right?" I asked. He looked a little pale.

"Nope," his voice was a little strained, breathy in that way that said he was either going to hurl or keel over. I quirked a brow.

"Not gonna get sick on me are you?" I asked. *He may be pretty, but I think my boy Aaron might be a bit of a wuss.*

"Nope, I just... I don't like needles," he confessed lamely. I burst out laughing.

"Well, too late now. You're in it to win it, my friend!" He smiled at me and nodded nervously. I went back to work. This was an easy piece, once the stencil was in place. I just needed to get it done. I worked in silence for a minute or two. I glanced up at Aaron's face and smiled. Yep. Endorphins had kicked in, he was getting into the zone a lot of people went into when they had ink done.

"Not so bad, is it?" I said softly.

"No, nuh uh. Not once you really get going," he agreed.

"So, what do you play?" I asked.

"Cello," he said.

"Get the fuck out!" I leaned back and looked him over to see if he was serious. He blinked.

"No, I'm being serious. I play the cello and the violin. Guitar sometimes, too." He smiled faintly.

"Never in a million years would have pegged you for a classical type. So what do you do for a living?" I asked, getting back into the tat.

"I play for the Philharmonic Orchestra," he said, and my eyebrows went up.

"No shit? You're that good?" I asked.

"Mmm hmm." He nodded and it jostled his arm. I pulled the gun away and looked. I was on a note, no harm done.

"Try not to move," I said.

"Sorry," he said. If he were any other guy, I would have been a dick and said, 'It's your tat' and shrugged it off, but I was liking Aaron, probably way more than I should.

"No worries, I just want it to look good for you, man." I glanced up into a startled expression. Aaron's face softened and he smiled, and I swallowed hard... Just something in his eyes...

"Thanks," he said.

"No problem." The buzz of my gun filled the ensuing silence. It took about ten minutes to finish him up. I slathered on the A&D and taped him up.

"You should leave this on for two hours. If the bandage is stuck, wet it. If you take a shower, avoid putting the tat directly under the spray for the first couple of days. Use Aquaphor to keep it moist..." I ran through aftercare instructions with him and he stared at me wide-eyed, and nodded. I handed them to him on a slip of paper and he smiled appreciatively.

"How much do I owe you?" he asked.

I stripped off my gloves and shrugged. What can I say, I wanted beautiful Aaron to remember me... That, and I was tired and feeling saucy. Wasn't like I was ever going to see him again.

"You know what, it's your first tat, it's late, and I think you're pretty. On the house," I told him and smiled big.

He laughed and grinned, "You think I'm pretty?" he asked incredulously. I quirked a brow and raised a shoulder in an indelicate shrug. If he were straight, he could take it as a joke; I'd used the right tone for it to be one. My heart seized in my chest at his next words.

"You're not so bad to look at yourself," he said and his voice had dipped, become husky with a lust of his own. I swallowed hard and stilled, eyeing him to see if he were fucking with me. His expression read stone-cold-serious.

Fuck. Me.

"Can I at least buy you a drink?" he asked, carefully. I found my traitorous body was on its own fucking program and my head nodding. *Too late for my mouth to deny him now.* I thought to myself. Not that I would deny Aaron my mouth, fuck, the exact opposite. I wanted to put my mouth anywhere and everywhere on his body that he'd let me. *What the fuck was wrong with me?*

"Yeah. I'd uh... I'd like that, Aaron." He smiled wide and stood up, pulling his sweater over his head.

"I know a great bar a few blocks over. Walk with me?"

I nodded dumbly.

"Yeah okay. Just let me clean up..."

What was I doing? This was so not the way to fly under the fucking radar! This could be a total disaster if any of the guys found out, so why was I taking such a huge risk?

My thoughts had been railing on this inner diatribe the entire time I'd cleaned up my area, through locking up the shop and they were pretty much on the same bent several minutes later as I walked along the cracked sidewalk beside Aaron. I had my hands stuffed into my jeans pockets and my leather jacket zipped against the mid-November chill. My prospect's cut blew back and open over the jacket, and I saw Aaron eye it out of the corner of his eye.

"So what else do you like aside from tattoos and Johnen Vasquez?" he asked and huddled into a leather bomber jacket of his own, his hands thrust deep into the pockets of it.

"Well, as you can probably tell, I'm trying to patch into the local MC."

He smiled. "I don't know many..." He cleared his throat, the pause pregnant. "Bikers," he finished. I sighed inwardly, catching his drift full on. He didn't know many gay bikers, and truth be told, neither did I, not a single damned one... I was so fucked.

"They don't know. I'm, um, careful about it." I swallowed the bitterness, and wondered why the hell I was telling him.

"Oh. I can't imagine that's good," he observed. I wanted to snort and say something snappy or sarcastic like 'No shit, Sherlock' but I didn't have it in me. Nor did I really have it in me to discuss the MC and my standing in it, at least not for right now. Don't get me wrong! I saw prospecting for the Sacred Hearts as a total labor of love. I loved the guys like they were my family and would do anything, and I do mean anything for them. But for tonight, right now, looking at Aaron with the perfect physique and those deep, soulful, liquid brown eyes, I just wanted to be me. The real me. No masks, no hiding, and believe me, I knew just how fucking dangerous that could be but for right now...

"Yeah, well, it's complicated," I said dryly, and he was as sharp as he was hot because he changed the subject, but not entirely so.

"So, was that your motorcycle back at the parlor?" Parlor? Who said 'parlor' anymore? I shook my head laughing softly.

"What, back at the shop?" I asked and smiled, teasingly. He smiled back and it made him devastatingly handsome.

"Yeah," he said shyly.

"Yeah, that was mine."

"What is it?" he bowed his head against the sharp autumn wind that cut in our direction and I admired his profile when he did it.

"She's a 1970 BMW 75/5," I answered.

"She?" He grinned and I shrugged.

"Meh they're like ships, they're all she's..."

"Does she have a name?" He held the door to the bar he'd suggested and I stopped.

"Not yet. Some of the other guys, their bikes have names."

I ducked inside. It was surprisingly mellow in here. Not loud at all.

Aaron grinned.

"Must be between sets," he muttered and I felt my brow wrinkle in confusion. He shrugged laconically, "Or it's a slow night."

"What're you talking about?"

His eyes widened and he pointed out the glass door. Shit! My eyes had been just for him; I hadn't noticed the sandwich board outside proclaiming loud and proud that it was Open Mic Night.

"Oh," I said, then muttered, "Wasn't looking at the damn sign."

Aaron smiled really wide and bit his lower lip to keep from laughing and I felt an answering grin of my own. I caught myself thinking, *damn! Never had a lip bite looked so fucking sexy before,* as we went into the bar, which wasn't really super crowded for a Thursday night. We found a table pretty easily and I took one of the tall stools.

"What're you drinking?" he asked.

"I'll just have a beer."

"Preference?"

"Surprise me."

He came back a few minutes later and set a bottle of Hefeweizen in front of me. He sat across from me and took a pull off his own.

"Thanks, man," I took a drink. Cold and crisp.

"So if you had to give her a name, what would you name her?" he asked and I smiled and laughed a little.

"No idea," I answered, honestly.

"Well, what did the other guys name theirs?" he asked.

I leaned back slightly and blew out a breath.

"Well, Dray, that's our VP, he named his bike 'Matilda', after his mother. Reaver calls his 'Baby' and Trig named his bike 'Betty' after the song." I took another sip of my beer and Aaron raised his bottle to his lips. *God I wanted to be that bottle.*

"What song?" Aaron frowned and I gave him a one-sided smile.

"Black Betty, it's an old song, but he took it from the more modern version by RamJam."

Aaron raised an eyebrow. "Never heard of them."

I grinned and brought out my phone. It was a good song and I happened to have it. I plugged in my headphones and handed him one side while I put the other in my ear and it almost felt like a modern version one of those old-ass Norman Rockwell paintings. You know, one of the ones of 1950's perfection where the dude and his date are sucking the same milkshake out of two different straws? I laughed and Aaron smiled, his brow furrowing in confusion.

"What's so funny?" he asked, and so I told him.

He laughed too, and asked softly, the smell of beer and spearmint faint on his breath, "Is that what this is? A date?"

I swallowed hard and licked my suddenly-dry lips. Aaron gasped faintly and I was startled to realize that he thought I was hot, which was, admittedly, a little weird for me. Not that he found me attractive as a dude, just... Most people were turned off by all the ink and piercings and I had a lot of both.

"Depends," I said, my voice faint. "Do you want it to be?" Aaron's deep dark eyes slid over my face, searching before he nodded slowly.

"Good song," he said, "Catchy, and a real good beat."

We listened to the rest of it, and he handed me back my earbud and leaned back. I suddenly missed the closeness. He smelled really nice. Like clean laundry, a mellow aftershave and that ever-present but faint tang of spearmint, which was only slightly out of harmony with the rest of him but still managed to fit.

We talked. A lot. Like a real damn lot, and Aaron was a cool fucking dude. The more he talked the more I liked him. And not just because he was my kind of hot. I think he liked me more than a bit too but I couldn't let myself be sure, at least not until I walked him a few more blocks to his place. He stopped in front of his apartment door and smiled at me. All of a sudden I realized, acutely, that we were alone. A frisson of anxiety travelled up my spine, his liquid dark eyes assessing through the lenses of his glasses. The faint light from his landing gleamed along the silver wire frames. I felt like my damned chest was going to cave in when he leaned towards me, deliberately, slowly... I couldn't stand it. I put my hands up, touching his face on either side gently and closed the gap between us.

Oh, god! His kiss was electric! His mouth was warm and his lips were soft and full beneath my own. I groaned and plunged my tongue past his lips. He tasted fresh and cool, like the beer we'd drunk overlaid by the sweet crisp zing of spearmint from the mint he'd sucked on the way from the bar. My dick got hard from it. Hell, I think I'd had a perpetual stiffy since he'd walked into the shop! He broke the kiss.

"Come inside," he breathed against my lips and I pulled back. Both of our chests were heaving. We'd kissed each other breathless. Fuck, I wanted to. I really wanted to.

"I don't do one-night-stands," I told him and flicked my tongue over suddenly-dry lips. He groaned and his mouth crashed against mine. We kissed savagely, needy, for several more moments before he broke away.

"Neither do I," he breathed.

"Pretty bad if we fuck on the first date," I said with a little self-deprecating smile. He smiled back.

"Who said anything about fucking? Maybe I just want to cuddle," he said with a rakish grin and I barked a laugh. I waved a hand, motioning for him to unlock the door. He did with shaking fingers.

"I'm serious, I don't do one-night-stands," I reiterated.

"I'm dead serious, too. Gimme your phone and I'll prove it." I went through the door behind him and he shut and locked it. I handed him my phone. He looked at me and frowned.

"Unlock it first, dork," he complained and I grinned, took it back and unlocked it, my thumb zipping over the screen. He added himself as a contact and handed it back. I raised an eyebrow and called the number. His phone started ringing; he smiled and pulled it out of his pocket.

"Okay, Aaron Cartwright. I believe you," I said glancing at the full name that he'd entered.

"Okay Andy..." he faltered, thumbs poised over his screen.

"Buchannan," I supplied, and smiling he typed it in and hit save.

"Good, now that we've got that out of the way..." he tossed his phone on a small table by the door, "kiss me," he demanded. Who the fuck was I to argue? For the next several minutes it was my mouth against his, our hands moving in a frantic dance to get each other out of our clothes.

Aaron lived in a small studio. A bed took up the vast majority of the room; he had a single folding chair, a stand for sheet music and sure enough, a cello and a guitar were propped to either side of it by the little apartment's only window. Thick drapes obscured that. Light glowed softly from a floor lamp by the bed, one of those halogen deals, and it was bright enough to see by, without being blinding. Pretty soon we were at the bed, the mattress hitting the backs of his thighs where I had him backed up to it. He reached out and the light from the floor lamp flared.

"I want to see you. All of you," he said against my mouth and I yanked his belt through the loops and let it fall. That sounded good to me; I wanted to see him right back! He started to pull my shirts, a thermal overlaid by a tee, off, over my head and I raised my arms to let him do it. I had a couple of necklaces on, just a couple of oddball things and they tumbled free, the cold metal resting against my chest. I jerked back from them and pulled them off, too, and dropped 'em. Aaron's eyes were roving over my tattoos. His fingertips lightly touched the zombified Little Mermaid Disney Princess on my ribs and I jerked, laughing.

"Ticklish?" he asked, a slow smile spreading on his lips, which were swollen from my kiss. He bit his lower lip, and Squick Jr. was standing straight at attention. I relieved him of his sweater and tee, and kissed and bit along the side of his neck and shoulder. He threw back his head and gasped out a lush moan as I let my fingers splay along the heated skin over his ribs. I pulled him tight against my body and groaned. He was so fucking beautiful, tight in all the right fucking areas!

"God, please tell me you like it all," I said against his neck.

"I want all of you," he said back, his voice brittle with desire. We made quick work of the rest of our clothes, and his fingers wrapped around my cock, stroking.

"Holy fuck!" I cried out, bowing my head. He turned me and pushed me down onto the bed and got to his knees between my own. He looked up my rainbow, tatted body and then looked at my cock.

"Never been with a man who's pierced," he said, fascinated. I smiled.

"I'm a night full of firsts then, aren't I?" I asked, and he smiled and took me into his hot, waiting mouth. I thought I'd fucking died and gone to heaven! Aaron had the most talented mouth... Holy God.

I bowed my head and closed my eyes and gave myself over to the sensation. He swirled his tongue around the head of my cock, teasing at my Prince Albert piercing, and I felt myself twitch. I had to fight myself to hold still, my hands clenched in the comforter to either sides of my hips as his head bobbed between my legs. He fondled my balls and I sucked in a sharp breath.

"Oh, fuck, yeah!" I threw back my head and moaned, and he must have liked what he heard, because he sucked me with more enthusiasm. I about lost my shit when he slipped his finger into my ass.

"Aaron! Aaron! I'm going to come!" I warned him, and he smiled around my cock in his mouth and worked at me harder.

"Oh shiiiiit!" I felt myself spill down his throat, and I couldn't help it, my hips bucked and I went deep, he swallowed and I could fucking feel his throat convulse around the tip of my head when he did it. I'd had a few decent blowjobs in my time, but fuck, he was, by far, the fucking best I'd ever had.

He sat back on his heels and smiled a secret little smile and watched me as I relearned how to breathe. I raked him with my gaze as he got up onto the bed, sitting beside me.

"You're good at that," I stated, and suddenly I couldn't wait to taste this beautiful man. He smiled and blushed faintly.

"Haven't had a whole lot of practice," he said, slightly embarrassed.

"Then that's one amazing natural talent," I told him, and reached for him. I kissed him and laid him back against the bed. He kissed me back with serious intensity. Truth was, I'd only been with one or two other guys, myself, and after that spectacular display, I was feeling some performance anxiety. I pulled back from the kiss and went down on him.

He was velvet-wrapped steel in my mouth. Not overly long, not overly thick, just a perfect size. I took him all the way in and I heard him pant. I rolled my eyes up his body and saw that he'd taken his glasses off. They were dangling, forlorn, against the bed in one outstretched hand. His other arm, the one with the bandage on it from the fresh ink I'd laid under his skin, was thrown over his eyes. I sucked him and his hips lifted off the bed.

"Oh, Andy," he groaned, my name an impassioned plea on those fucking perfect lips of his. I smiled around him. He tasted so good, masculine but sweet at the same time. I backed off of him and plunged him deep; the tip of him barely hit the back of my throat but was in the prime spot for my gag reflex. I fought it down and breathed with minor difficulty around him and laved the underside of his cock with my tongue. He moaned and it was his turn to fight the urge to writhe.

I felt myself getting hard again. I wanted to fuck him so bad it wasn't even funny. I pulled off of him.

"I've got condoms in the headboard," he said, as if he'd read my mind, and indicated a cubby in his headboard with a wave of his glasses.

"You going to let me fuck you?" I asked, and he nodded. I reached into the indicated cubby, fished around, and pulled out a condom and a small bottle of lube.

"Fucking Boy Scout. too, I love it," I said and he laughed. I tore open the foil packet and rolled the condom on, and he watched me do it, his expression hungry and full of desire. I dripped lube onto my cock and coated it with my hand. The best fucking sex I'd ever had was messy as hell, but I had a feeling the top spot was about to be taken with this right here with Aaron. I wanted to watch his face while I fucked him, so I wouldn't let him turn over. I got between his thighs and put his hands on his ass cheeks. He held them apart for me and I lubed up his asshole, sliding first one then two of my long fingers into him to the second knuckle.

His eyes slipped shut and his cheeks held a faint pink blush that made me throb with need. I moved my fingers after he was good and slick. I pressed the head of my condom-covered cock to his ass and felt him push out to accept me. I closed my eyes and reveled in the sensation of breeching his opening. His ass spasmed around me and I bowed my head and pressed in harder and deeper, until I was balls-fucking-deep.

"Fuuuuck you're tight," I said, and my voice sounded breathless, even to me. I pressed my palms to the backs of his thighs up near his knees, holding his legs out of my way and slowly drew back then pressed forward. He moaned, the look on his face pure ecstasy, and it nearly tipped me over the edge. I took my time with him, enjoying every minute. It'd been a long time since I'd been able to let loose and enjoy myself so completely.

I looked up the long, lean line of Aaron's torso and smiled, picking up the pace. His cock was swollen, high and tight to his body, the head riding just below his bellybutton, smooth and perfect and just plain beautiful to look at. I gave myself over to all the myriad sensations of his body. The warmth and heat, the feel of him squeezing around my cock, the crisp hair of his thighs under my palms and I came, hard, after several long minutes inside him. Shit, who am I kidding? I lost myself in Aaron so completely I couldn't tell you for how long, could have been a couple of minutes, it could have been an hour, I just don't know.

I let him go and slid from him, bowing over him, my forehead coming to rest over his heart. His fingers tangled in my lengthening hair gone too long between cuts, running through it so gently, delicately pulling and working through any tangles that he encountered. His touch was tender.

"Mmmm, does this mean it's my turn?" I heard the lazy, satiated smile in his voice and felt my lips curve into one of my own against his skin.

"Hell, yes," I said. He untangled himself from beneath me and put on a condom. "How do you want me?" I asked.

"On your knees," he murmured. I was a fan of doggy-style, so I complied. He lubed me up gently and competently, and I relaxed and let him do his thing, giving myself over to him. He pushed into me and I groaned. He felt a lot bigger this way than he had in my mouth.

"Oh, God, harder," I gasped, and he groaned and complied. Shit, fuck, and God damn! He was perfect. I pressed back onto his cock, meeting him with every thrust as he pounded my ass. After a time he moaned and his voice, high and tight with passion, warned me he was close, which made me smile. I wanted him to come and he did, jerking hard against my body, his long hands with their broad palms stroking up and down my back, smoothing over the colored skin.

"I love the colors," he gasped, and placed a few kisses to my inked skin, almost reverently. I smiled into the comforter and he pulled out of me, I shuddered, so satisfied. He felt so good.

"Thanks," I murmured. We cleaned up; I helped him with his new tattoo. We took our time, making out in his almost-too-small-for-the-both-of-us shower. His kiss was patient and kind, as he explored my mouth with his, more thoroughly than anyone else ever had.

"Stay the night?" he asked timidly, and I nodded and pressed my forehead to his, cupping his cheeks with my hands and reveling in the sensation of his lean hard body against mine.

"Sure, yeah."

He laughed. "Isn't there some kind of rule against sex on the first date?" he queried and I scoffed.

"I'm a biker," at least I hoped to be... "Don't you know? The rules don't fucking apply to us," I joked. He laughed and we got out of the shower and dried each other off. We cuddled up in his bed, which was a hell of a lot more comfortable than the crappy futon back at my place and I fell asleep to Aaron's soft and even breathing, the weight of his head and arm across my chest and stomach oddly comforting in the close dark.

All I could think was *how was I going to do this?* Balancing the MC and my day job was hard enough. How the fuck was I gonna add a boyfriend to the mix? I didn't know, but Aaron made me really, really want to try. I was just that damned attracted to him and I really wanted to see where it could go.

Fuck.

Way to make things more complicated.

2

____

S quick...

"Good morning." Aaron's lush mouth curved into a gentle smile. I sucked in a deep breath and exhaled in a rush to clear out the cobwebs. I stretched and flicked my tongue over my dry lower lip and clipped the edge of the ring through the lower left corner of it. I stretched hard, cat-like, and returned Aaron's smile with a faint one of my own.

"Morning," I replied, my voice rough with sleep, and asked, "What time is it?"

"Early yet, and time for us to talk." The ominous nature of his statement was belied by the smile still firmly in place on his face.

"Yeah?"

"Yeah."

I eyed him carefully. "What'cha got?" I asked, and steeled myself for whatever he was about to say.

"I want to see you again," he said carefully, his gaze fixed on his beautiful hands which rested on his white down comforter.

The hard look I'd been giving him softened.

"I'd like that," I reached out brightly colored fingers and lightly touched his face. His eyes snapped up to mine and I leaned forward and brushed my lips across his. His eyes slipped shut and he kissed me back.

"I don't know how to do this, Aaron," I said after we'd broken apart. I closed my eyes with shame and turned my head, swallowing hard.

"Tell me," he said softly, and settled back into the softness of his bed, his calloused fingertips trailing against my skin, his liquid brown eyes roving the images inked underneath, picking out different things from the myriad mash of colors. I closed my eyes again and relished the simple touch. I didn't get touched very often and this... This was nice.

"Andy?" His voice broke me out of the comfortable silence; his fingertips withdrew and I opened my eyes.

"Don't stop." I pleaded. "I'm just trying to figure out where to start."

He frowned slightly and nodded, his fingertips sliding down my arm, over my hip and back up, "I've never seen someone as tattooed as you," he murmured.

"I knew I was different in about the fourth or fifth grade," I whispered. "While most of the other boys were starting to notice Nikki Stratford's budding tits, I was noticing how well Michael Donovan was filling out through the shoulders. It only got worse. I was into choir while the rest of the dudes were getting into sports. I liked drama and art class, and the name-calling started." My voice hitched. These were not my favorite moments of history to relive. Like, at all.

"I was fifteen when I came out to my parents and my dad first kicked my ass and then kicked my ass out." Aaron made a sympathetic noise and I shook my head. "Don't, don't do that. I don't want to be pitied," I said, and my voice came out harsher than I meant it to. Aaron cupped my face in his hands and forced me to look at him.

"Sympathize? Yes. Empathize? Yes. Pity you? What for?" he smiled and the tightness in my chest eased.

"What about you?" I asked, needing to get the topic of conversation off of me for a minute.

"About the same. I managed to hide it for the most part. I played baseball, took a girlfriend, went through the motions until I moved away from home. Got into college and everything is different in college." He smiled like I should know, and I shook my head. He looked surprised.

"Dad kicked my ass out when I was fifteen, remember?" I fixed Aaron with a steady gaze as I continued, "Disowned me, told my mother and my sister I was dead to them. I had this friend in high school, my only friend really, Sarah Warren. She and her mom took me in. Let me sleep on their couch for a while but Sarah's mom was barely making ends meet. I tried to get out and find a job. Had to drop out of school... My art was what kept me going. I would draw as a way to escape." I closed my eyes, this next bit was a bitch to talk about.

"When it got cold, I would beg for enough change... I needed a buck-twenty-four. A buck-twenty-four was my ticket to paradise, man. There was this shitty fucking diner and a buck-twenty-four would buy me a bottomless cup of coffee. It not only warmed me up, but gave me a warm place to sit all day and helped when I got hungry. I learned pretty damned quick to lie my fucking ass off when somebody asked my age. I was fifteen fucking years old," I scrubbed my face with my hands, breathed deep and breathed out.

I had done some shit, a lot of shit, that I am just plain not fucking proud of, back then, just to survive. You get fucking hungry enough or cold enough you'd do just about anything. I'd had to hustle, fucking steal, fight my way out of more situations... I'd done just about every drug known to man, just to fucking forget where I was, who I was, what I was, that had landed me in some of the shittiest fucking places. I didn't want to think about it. I didn't even fucking know why I was telling Aaron any of this... other than he was the first, and only, person I had never lied to, and I didn't want to start now.

"You don't have to tell me any more right now," he started when I'd been silent too long, "I just... I just want to know you, Andy; you're different than anyone else I've ever met. Truer, more honest, somehow," he looked at me, his eyes bright, and I scoffed. If only he knew how fucking far off the mark he was.

"I like you, Aaron. Don't know what it is about you, but you're fucking electric," I told him and he smiled. We kissed and that charge thrilled through my lips and went straight to my cock.

"Make you breakfast?" he asked softly, against my mouth.

"I'd like that," I said and let him go.

"Stay there, I want you to be comfortable, and after last night, I think you've earned breakfast in bed." I laughed and couldn't help my mind drifting back to his talented mouth on my cock, which stirred some more beneath his covers.

I watched him move naked around his kitchen, which admittedly I couldn't see much of, between the counter and the cupboards that hung from the ceiling, but it was enough. He fixed us some ham-and-cheese omelets and some toast, and joined me back in the bed.

"Thanks," I said appreciatively. I caught his eyes roaming over my ink again and I couldn't blame him. I was a riot of color. My arms both had full sleeves; the backs of my hands were done too. It looked like I wore fingerless gloves of ink, the knuckles of my fists tattooed with elaborate letters on the right fist spelling 'Love' and on my dominant hand, the left, 'Pain'. My back was completely done; so was my ass. Both legs were fully sleeved too, right down to the tops of my feet. I had tattoos painting my ribs all the way up. Both sides of my neck done, too.

Most of my ink was bastardized versions of children's cartoons. I had a zombified Little Mermaid on the left side of my ribs, her tail half rotted away, and I had an image of Snow White ball-gagged and pulling a train of the Seven Dwarves over my right hip, curving around onto my back.

I had an image of Cinderella on my thigh, with a black eye and fat lip and the caption 'When did he stop treating you like a princess?' underneath her in flowing script that was almost swallowed by the next image. My skin had become a patchwork of a broken childhood and just generally fucked-up images, images meant to evoke feelings of discomfort. It's only part of what earned me the nickname Squick, and I could see the question in Aaron's eyes.

"Go ahead and ask," I said softly.

"Your skin is beautiful, so many bright colors... but some of the images are so..."

"Vile? Fucked-up? Squicky?" I supplied, when he'd fallen quiet, trying to come up with a word that described them that wouldn't be offensive.

"Yes. Those, too, but also thought-provoking, and beautiful in their own right, and not all of them are... messed up. Just, I guess, why?" He continued to look, fingertips brushing a rose on my arm that curved around a white Phantom of the Opera mask with a French flag behind it. The image was small and sat on the rounded bone of my wrist. It had hurt like a bitch but it was Ashton's tattoo and had been worth it when Zander had done it for me.

She had the same small image inked on the back of her right shoulder. Her first tattoo, it had been done by Trig and was all her idea. She'd asked me to draw it for her, though, and I'd been so honored. About a week after Trig had put it on her, (because let's face it, if anyone was going to put ink under Ashton's skin it was going to be him) I'd had Zander do the same image on me. Ashton had almost cried when I'd shown her. She was thrilled at us having matching tattoos, Thank fuck. I was half-afraid she'd be upset at not having an original to her piece, but nope. Not Sunshine. Generous to the last, that was her.

I thought about what Aaron was asking me, and played with my lip ring, flicking it back and forth with the tip of my tongue as I contemplated the best way to answer him.

It had started when I was sixteen with the Johnny the Homicidal Maniac tattoo. I related to the character. Nny was fucked-up in the head, but it was beyond his control. After my dad kicked my ass out, I pretty much felt like I was on the same wavelength.

"When I started getting ink done, I felt like Nny. Fucked-up in the head for being gay, but at the same time like it was beyond my control. You know? What I did have control over was what I put under my skin and I guess that just kind of came out. I just got this affinity for images that were fucked-up, a twisting of something inno-cent. So, after getting all of the JTHM characters in one place or another, I just kind of moved on to other cartoon characters." I shrugged.

"Not going to lie, Andy, I was really entertained by the dead Mickey Mouse in the rat trap on your ass. I thought it was pretty funny," he admitted.

I laughed and hugged Aaron to me.

"Of all of 'em that's your favorite huh?" I asked.

"I didn't say that! I haven't seen them all to decide on which one is my favorite. You'll just have to come back tonight, so I can look at them all." He gave me a cheeky grin.

"Tonight, huh?" I asked, and rubbed a hand up and down the ink-free skin down the middle of my chest and stomach.

"Yeah."

"I work tonight," I reminded him.

"Come by after." His tone was eager and brooked no argument. I laughed.

"I don't know," I teased and then sobered a bit. "Club business could come up."

"Well, if it doesn't," he prompted.

"I'll be here," I said, and the smile that graced his lips was worth it. He kissed me, and then he went to work with that talented mouth of his.

God, he was phenomenal, but all too soon we had to shower and get dressed. He had to get to practice and I had to get back to my bike and ride home for a change of clothes before the shop opened for the day. As I left him at his bus stop, I couldn't help but feel so many things all at once. Excited, troubled, exhilarated, scared, to name a few. Anxiety gnawed at me. I sighed, as I swung a leg over my bike.

It was probably best just to see where things would go, to not overthink it and to just enjoy what stolen moments I could have with Aaron because I had to face it; the club came first, before anything. I'd worked too hard to stop now, and I wasn't going to, which meant that my time with Aaron was limited.

I was afraid the guys would find out. Seeing the looks of disgust and disappointment like I'd seen on my family's face? Well, I didn't want to face that from the only other family I'd ever known since. Trig and Zander were good guys. They'd hired me, knowing I was hooked on drugs, put up with me flaking, and kept my clients safe when I was too high to hold a gun steady. They helped me, guided me; they shaped me into a phenomenal tattooist, picking up where Rusty left off. God love that man.

I owed Rusty for taking a chance on me in the first place. The old school and just plain old tattoo artist had seen my drawings in my sketchbook at the café I used to camp out in when the weather was shit. He started talking to me, put me up in a room in the back of his shop, started mentoring me. He knew damn well I wasn't eighteen. He had me clean up the shop, got me a fake ID in case anyone came around asking, went to my folks' place and strong-armed the important papers I'd need to get around in life from them. You know, my birth certificate, my social security card... those things. I still don't know how he found out about my parents or where they were but my dad must have told him I was a fag or some shit.

Rusty had come into the shop with a manila file folder with my papers in it. Then he had told me point-blank he didn't care if I sucked dick or liked having my ass reamed, just not to do it around his shop. Then, he just handed over my stuff and we never spoke on it again and I just sort of fell into the groove of don't ask/don't tell. Rusty died suddenly in his sleep a year or two later, but not before teaching me how to drive, how to fix my own car, how to tattoo and most importantly, how to survive. I mean, I knew how to fight, I'd pretty much had to figure that shit out on my own as a matter of necessity, but Rusty, he taught me how to do it better. He taught me how to fight dirtier and he taught me how to not to give a fuck about whoever it was I was facing off against.

In the year-and-a-half or so with Rusty, I learned more about life and survival than in all my years living under my parent's roof. Rusty was like the father I always should have had. When he died the bank foreclosed on his shop and I was cast adrift again, only this time I had a car to live out of for the meantime and a fucking bank account with some cash in it. Not only that, I had a couple of marketable skills.

I found an ad in the paper that Open Road Ink was opening and needed a New-School artist, so I went in. Zander looked over my stuff and handed it off to Trig, who took one look at me, instead of my art, and asked me what I was on. I didn't try to bullshit him. I told him I was tweaking. They helped me get my shitty apartment by being references. Trig, who's intimidating as fuck on a good day, and wasn't having many of those back then, told me if I fucked him, he'd fuck me back harder, and the rest is history.

I went into my apartment and threw some clothes into a backpack along with my good art pencils and sketchbook and checked the time. Shit. Four missed calls from Zander. I hadn't remembered putting my phone on silent. I called him back.

"What's up?" I asked as soon as he answered.

"Nothin' now, got it handled. Where the fuck were you?" he asked.

"Nowhere, sleeping, didn't realize I had my phone on silent," I lied and he grunted.

"Yeah, bullshit. Your bike was outside the shop. False alarm last night, fucking system was on the fritz again and you live closer. Tried to get you to go out there and check on it. I ended up going," he said.

"Oh." I didn't have a clever comeback for that one.

"So, seriously, where were you?" he asked, curiosity lacing his tone.

"Went out drinkin' with a buddy of mine, racked out on his couch," I said.

"Mmm," he grunted, "Why didn't you just say so, kid?"

"I'm hung over, and it ain't yer business?" I tried, and he laughed.

"You asking me or telling me, Squickie, m'boy?" I hung my head and rubbed the back of my neck.

"I'm fucking telling you, douchebag! Is that better?" The smile in my voice took a lot of any bite that would have been in it right out. Zander's laugh boomed over the phone and I grinned.

"All right man, you keep your secrets, even though you don't have to," he wheezed out, and I grimaced. "I'll see you in a few."

"Yeah, be right there," I said, and we hung up. If only he knew just how much I needed to keep my secrets, and how many there were, I mean, honestly.

I changed into clean clothes so I wasn't wearing what I'd been in yesterday and took off. It was getting cold for the bike, but my car wasn't running and I didn't exactly have time to fix the damned thing. Even less now, so the old Mazda got to just sit for now. The ride to the shop was brisk. I backed my bike into the parking stall next to Zander's and shut it off. I went in, helmet in hand and nodded to the man himself, behind the counter.

"What's up?" I asked.

"Another day, another dollar," he grunted. I nodded.

"Sorry about last night, man," I told him. I mean, shit, friendship aside, he was still my boss.

"No worries, you got a life too. Glad to see you gettin' out." He was counting out the till, getting it ready for the day, the green bills sliding through his thick fingers as he made the count. When my phone buzzed in my pocket, I slipped it out of my jeans.

Aaron: Miss U already. Is that lame?

I smiled.

Me: I don't think so. I'm thinking about you too. How's the tat?

"Man, what's got you smiling?" Zander asked, pausing in the middle of the five-dollar bills. He raked me over with his gaze, a wicked grin quirking up one side of his mouth.

"Just someone I met last night. It's nothing," I shoved my phone in my pocket but he'd gotten that wicked gleam in his eye, the one that was pure Zander and made him look like a dog who'd just found his new favorite bone.

"Seriously. Who?" he asked.

"Nobody!" I lied and rolled my eyes. He chuckled as I made my way across the black-and-white checkered linoleum, past the red-and-black painted walls, down the black hallway with the framed newspaper articles about the shop and into the riot of color that was my space.

I didn't do framed photos. My art went right up on the walls. I had two walls with my special brand of New-School art mural-style on them. The third, at the back, with my drafting table pushed up against it, was white. It fluttered with like a million drawings and stencils that had been taped haphazardly to it above and all around my desk. The fourth wall wasn't even a wall. It was a half wall with a space cut into it to walk into my area. I put my helmet on the shelf under my drafting table and slid my backpack next to it.

I slipped my phone out of my pocket, dying to read the message that had come in on it while Zander was looking at me like I was his next challenge. The dude had to know everything but he was quiet about it. He'd watch, and hunt, and peck it out of you when you least expected the questions to come in. He was pretty decent at busting down walls, the problem was he wasn't always subtle about it, or didn't care to be. Zander had a temper, too, which wasn't always fun to deal with. Still. All the way around, he was a cool dude.

Aaron: Itchy

Me: That means it's dry. Is it scaled looking?

I frowned. I'd given him a tube of Aquaphor that had been living in my jacket pocket. I always had the stuff laying around, with as much and as often as I had my shit touched up.

Aaron: A little.

I sighed and smiled a little to myself. It was his first tattoo. He didn't know.

Me: You got the stuff I gave you?

Aaron: Yeah I put some on this morning.

Me: Put some more on.

Aaron: Already!?

Me: You're past due.

Aaron: I thought it was a once or twice a day thing.

Me: Every time it gets dry. Trust me. I'm a professional.

Aaron: LOL Okay. Have a good day. I have to go in to practice now. See you tonight?

Me: Barring any club business, yes.

Aaron: :-*

Me: WTF is that?

Aaron: A kiss.

Me: Oh. LOL I'll save mine for when I see you in person.
Aaron: K!

The bell over the shop door rang and my head jerked up, startled. Zander, at the entry of my cubicle, cursed. I frowned.

"What the fuck, over?" I asked.

"Was gonna try and sneak up on you and snatch it. Seriously, who is it? What's her name?"

I scowled deeply.

"What are you? Twelve?" I demanded, and shoved my phone back in my hip pocket. Zander grinned a broad grin and bobbed his head in an erratic nod that made him look like a fucking bobble head doll.

"Just leave it alone," I grumbled.

"Leave what alone?" Ashton's voice was close, and it was Zander's turn to startle. He whirled and she was right behind him. I smirked at her from behind his back. Zander had a hand to his broad chest.

"Jesus, Sunshine! Make some fucking noise next time!" She wrinkled her nose and gave Zander an impish grin.

"Stop picking on my shop bestie!" she said and Zander laughed.

"You're getting a brass pair," Zander remarked, shaking his head, and again Ashton's nose wrinkled, this time in distaste. Zander's laugh boomed out into the shop and Ashton moved aside so that he could go past her. She gave me a sad, knowing smile and ghosted off in Trig's direction; he stood just inside the door talking on his own phone, his eyes tracking his woman's movements, a mixture of love, concern and confusion in them.

Our eyes met and he nodded in my direction; I gave him a guarded one back. He didn't understand my relationship with Sunshine. Never had, but, I think, on some instinctual level he knew I wasn't any kind of threat, so he didn't feel the need to question it. Thank fuck. I shrugged out of my jacket and startled a bit when Trig's voice rose.

"We aren't paying for shit! Now, I don't know how many times we've had to come out here in the middle of the night because your fucking alarm goes off for no goddamned reason! No! I will not calm the fuck down! This has been a pain in our ass for long enough, we are way past me being calm about it." I could almost hear the big man grinding his teeth from here.

Ashton was near him and gingerly put her arms around his hips, tucking herself into his side. He shuddered and the tension just eased out of him, melting off of him into the floor. It made me smile.

"Yes. You do that," he bit into the phone, and it looked like he wanted to throw it. He shoved it in his jacket pocket beneath his cut and put his arms around Sunshine.

"Sorry, Baby," he murmured and she looked at him with nothing short of adoration.

"It's okay," she murmured back.

The alarm company was becoming more of a hassle than a boon lately with three, sometimes four, false alarms a month happening. It was enough to make us a little crazy, especially because when the cops got called by the alarm company to come check it out, we had to pay a fee to the county. I tore myself away from the scene Ashton and Trig were making, in a bid to give them some privacy. I didn't see Trig lose his cool very often, even less in the time that he'd been with Ashton. Things were just tense all the way around, since July. The Suicide Kings had been laying low and we were all getting a bit nervous. The shit would go down eventually, we just didn't know how, or when, or what it would be, or even what it could be, and it was anybody's guess.

I brought out my pencils and sketch pad and settled at my drafting table. I didn't have any clients today, so instead I set myself up to work on some of my drawings for upcoming tats. Tattooing wasn't all about laying ink under skin. The designs had to come from somewhere; custom pieces took time to draw, sometimes hours. That sixty-five-dollar tattoo that took an hour to ink in was usually more like four, five, or maybe even six hours of work, drawing, and shading, and re-drawing. That part of the process the clients rarely, if ever, saw, especially when it came to the more elaborate pieces.

So when it was 'slow' in the shop, it wasn't really, because I had drawings to do. Not only that, if the shop was busy, then so was I. Getting interrupted fifty million times while trying to draw a piece was a bitch, too, but I couldn't gripe because usually the interruption meant rent for next month or food for next week, and the rat race went on.

Today was no exception. I got two pieces done, and was interrupted something like fifty times. Add to that, Zander had a screamer in his piercing room; by the time Trig was pulling the cord on the 'Open' sign to turn it off, I wanted to scream myself. I stared at my phone for long minutes and waited for it to betray me with a call from the club, but it remained silent and dark. Thank fuck. I really wanted to see Aaron.

I was shoving my pencils back in their case and missed Zander coming into my space. I was too damned preoccupied with thoughts of Aaron's talented mouth on my cock to pay my boss and fellow prospect much mind. He snatched my phone off the table and I smirked. It was locked. He dropped it back onto my table with a mock pouty-face and picked up my open backpack off the chair, peering into it.

"You're not going home!" he crowed excitedly. I rolled my eyes in exasperation and took my pack, shoving my sketchpad and pencils into it.

"Just, give it up, man," I groaned.

"Nah, you present a mystery, and I just have to solve it." He clapped me on the back.

"Dude, we've known each other pushing four maybe five years! You already know everything there is to know." I pulled on my jacket and cut, and Zander raised a scarred eyebrow.

"Don't think so, Squick. You play your cards close to the vest." He held up a hand to stop me from speaking when I opened my mouth to argue. "Not sayin' it's a bad thing, dude! I know where you come from. I'm still not sure how you got there, but that's a puzzle for another day. I like you, kid, you're one of my brothers. What you see as me bugging the hell out of you is really me checking up on you and making sure you're straight and don't need any help. You never ask for it, so sometimes we gotta make sure. You dig?" He tilted his head and speared me with his gaze.

"I get you," I said reluctantly, "Still, who I am and am not fucking is none of your business."

Zander grinned real wide, and I cursed myself inwardly for making such a rookie mistake.

"So you –are– getting some! Attaboy!" He turned to go. "Gonna find out who, eventually," he called over his shoulder. As I watched his retreating back as he went back up front, my phone buzzed across the table with a text alert. I caught it as it slipped off the edge.

Aaron: See you soon. Is it retarded that I feel this excited?

I smiled to myself.

Me: If it is then we ride the short bus together.

I got the hell out of the shop while the getting was good and rode the six or seven blocks to Aaron's apartment. By the time I finished climbing the stairs and was walking down the long open-air landing, his door was open, spilling a rectangle of light into the crisp dark.

"I've been wanting to do this all day," he said, pulling me into his apartment by the lapels of my jacket. He swung the door shut and as soon as it was, his mouth was on mine.

I dropped my pack to the floor and kissed him back. His hands smoothed up my chest and cupped my face. I slipped mine under his shirt and he jerked in my grasp, crying out at my cold hands on his heated skin. I touched him everywhere; he laughed and tried to pull out of my hands, but nuh-uh. No way was I letting him get away. I bit his lower lip, and he gasped and stopped struggling. My hands warmed quickly, and so did the fires of the extreme lust going on between us.

I shoved Aaron to his knees and gasped, "I want your mouth on me. Now."

He smiled up at me from the floor and eagerly worked at the front of my pants. I groaned at the image and stood, my hips jolting as his hot, wet mouth took me in to the hilt. Fuck, I liked that. I liked him. What the fuck was I going to do?

3

____

S quick...

"My mom was cool," Aaron was saying. "I knew there was something different about me, she knew it, too. It wasn't just the music, I mean I'm the son of a public school music teacher and a music theory professor." He scoffed, "My being musically-inclined was to be expected."

"It was other things. Guys started going apeshit over a girl in a short skirt and me... I couldn't stop looking at my best friend, Bruce." He cuddled in closer to me and I held him a little tighter. We'd been talking for a couple of hours, maybe more, since our wild passion-explosion after I'd come through the door.

"Yeah?" I prompted, when he'd been quiet a moment too long.

"I lost my friendship with him over it. It was in high school, our senior year." He sighed and the sound held the weight of his pain.

"I hid it all through college, even though I didn't have to. For a while I was ashamed, you know?" He looked up at me but I stayed silent. Stiff. He nodded carefully. "Of course, you know," he said softly.

"Yeah," I affirmed.

"What are you going to do?" he asked quietly, when the silence had stretched too long again. I worried my lip ring back and forth with my tongue, delaying my inevitable answer.

"I don't know," I said honestly. "I like you a lot. I want to see where this goes, but I can't keep you a secret. It wouldn't be fair or right of me to ask that of you, so I'm not..." I paused to gather my thoughts, changing my trajectory mid-sentence. "At the same time, I can't lie to the guys forever. They're going to find out." I pressed the heel of my hand against my eye, where a headache was starting. I was worrying myself fucking sick.

"I know the results are unpredictable, but still, wouldn't it be better to come clean before they found out? Tell on yourself, before someone else tells on you?" he asked. I looked down into those beautiful liquid dark eyes and let out a breath I hadn't realized I'd been holding.

"Probably," I agreed. "I'm pretty sure I'm going to have my ass handed to me..." I swallowed hard. I didn't think they'd kill me. In fact, I knew for sure they wouldn't, but the thought of any one of them turning their backs on me, of doing to me what my dad had done to me, of seeing the raw naked disappointment, or worse, disgust in any of their eyes... Well, let's just say that for me, there were some things worse than death. I'd rather feel the kiss of Reaver's blades, than see any of those things on Trig or Zander's faces.

"I don't want to lose my job," I said lamely.

"I know they're your friends, but if they're really your friends, they wouldn't do that to you. If they do, I know it will hurt, but you're talented, Andy." He rubbed his fingers across an image in my sketchpad, which was splayed across his lap.

"You'll find another job, but wouldn't it be nice to be free? To be who you are on the inside on the outside, too, all of the time and not just behind locked doors?" His words were both true and really fucking enticing. I tipped his chin up with gentle fingers just the little bit more I needed to claim his mouth with mine.

Maybe Aaron coming into my life was just the push I needed, at the time I needed it. I couldn't let them patch me in to the club living the lie I was living. Brotherhood was more than just about having each other's backs in a fight or a bind. It was about honesty and being true to each other. No secrets, no judgment. It was about having each other's backs no matter what, not just when it suited you. Aaron and I had been talking about it for quite some time through the euphoric haze of our post-sex blissed-out state. I'd told him all about the guys, about some of the bikes, and about the girls too. I think he liked Ashton already. She had that kind of effect on people.

"I know I can't hide forever," I said plaintively. "Still doesn't mean I know what I'm going to do."

Aaron nodded and opened his mouth to speak, but my phone started buzzing across the night table. I reached over and plucked it off the tabletop and groaned.

"Dray," I said, and Aaron made a motion with his long fingers, zipping across his lush lips, locking them up and throwing away the key. It was fucking endearing and adorable. I answered the phone with an appreciative smile.

"Yo."

"Prospect. What're you doing?" he asked.

"Stuff. What do you need?"

Dray snorted, "Closed-mouthed bastard. Can you interrupt whatever it is and go get Ghost?" I sat up straighter.

"What's wrong with Ghost?" I asked, concerned.

"Down at The Spot, drunk off his ass. Too drunk to drive. He's flyin' colors, so the bar owner called me. I gotta be up early to get my girl and me to work. This type of shit is what you happy bastards are for." I could hear the grin in his voice. It was pretty safe to assume that the 'happy bastards' were me and Zander, the club's two prospects.

"I'm on it, boss, except I don't have a car right now. My Mazda is dead in my driveway, I haven't fixed it yet," I said, and swung my legs over the side of the bed.

"I think Ghost has his truck out there. Just get a ride. You're a big boy, Prospect, fucking figure it out." Dray grunted and held his hand over the phone, or just held it away from his face, because I heard a muffled "Fuck, baby, that's nice!" and suddenly I couldn't get off the fucking phone fast enough.

"Got it. No problem, have a good time, Dray." I heard him bark a laugh and the call disconnected. I sighed.

"Come on, I'll give you a ride out there and drop you off. You can come back and get your bike after work tomorrow night." Aaron captured his lower lip between his teeth in a bid to squash his devilish grin.

"Gonna hold my girl hostage on me, huh?" I asked, and pushed him back into the sheets and kissed him breathless.

He laughed.

"I think I would do just about whatever it took to see you again. I like your company, and the sex isn't half-bad either."

I laughed and gave him a peck on the nose, his words suffusing me with a warm glow.

"Come on. I have to go bail my brother out of trouble," I made a sour face. "Hopefully it'll be just that, and not 'out of jail'." The thought spurred me in to action. I did a quick rinse-off in the shower, two minutes or less. While I was drying off, Aaron appeared in the bathroom doorway in some loose sweats, sneakers on his feet and a set of car keys in his hand.

"Where is this place?" he asked.

"You know The Spot Bar and Grill on the main drag in Old Town?" I asked, pulling on my jeans.

"That the sports place?"

"Yeah." I pulled my discarded shirts over my head then sat on the edge of the bed and put my socks and All-Stars on.

"Sure. Want me to drop you off just up the block?"

I froze and looked at Aaron's face, which was carefully-guarded. He had that look like he was steeling himself to be hurt, and while I wasn't ready to jump out of the closet draped in a rainbow flag and throwing glitter while singing at the top of my lungs in falsetto... I couldn't do it to him. I couldn't ask him to do that.

"I don't know what the fuck I'm going to do about my situation, but I know what I'm not going to do. I'm not going to treat you like some dirty little secret, Aaron. That shit fucking –hurts–. My folks did it for years." I shook my head, "No, fuck that. You can drop me off out front."

I stood up and pulled on my jacket and cut and slung my backpack over my shoulder. I'd need the clean clothes if I was going to drunk-sit. Might get in the line of fire by accident, if Ghost felt like puking. I turned to look at Aaron and the look he was giving me said it all: grateful. Other emotions roiled in the liquid depths of his eyes, too, but I didn't have time to figure them out.

"Is it cool if I leave my helmet with you, too?" I asked. He nodded mutely. I wanted him to know that I wanted to see him, despite the fucked-up situation I had myself in. If I left my helmet, I had to come back to his door. His willingness to keep it for me spoke volumes on its own.

"Come on, before your friend... er, brother, gets himself into more trouble than it sounds like he's already in." I nodded and followed him out behind the building. He unlocked the doors on his older, little Subaru, a bubble-backed station wagon thing, and we got inside. I sighed.

"I'd much rather be back in bed with you," I grumbled as he started the car. He smiled at me, the glare on his lenses from the overhead street light through the windshield hiding his eyes from me.

"I don't disagree," he said, and shifted the car into reverse. We spent the short trip into Old Town in silence, his hand on my thigh, my hand curled around his long fingers.

4

S quick...

The inside of the bar was dark and surprisingly crowded. I glanced at the banks of televisions and realized it was a game-night. I scanned the murky interior and landed on the familiar Sacred Hearts colors at the end of the bar. The bartender caught my eye and gestured slightly, indicating I should meet him down the bar some. I went, and he stuck out his hand.

"Jimmy Mac," he said, I took his hand and shook. "Dragon send you?" he asked. I shook my head.

"Dray! Our VP!" I called, over the sudden, loud, cheering. Jimmy nodded and leaned over the bar. He was an older guy with long graying hair in a loose ponytail down his back. He wore a black tee shirt with the bar's logo on it and a pair of faded jeans. He held a dishrag in his hand and picked up a glass to polish it.

"Your boy's been drowning his sorrows hard over there for the last two hours. I got his keys. He handed 'em over without a fight." He produced a set of keys from his pocket and handed them to me.

"Thanks," I called.

"Don't mention it. You guys have helped me and mine out before. I don't mind giving back." He nodded at me and I gave him a respectful nod back. I went over to Ghost and slid up onto the stool next to him. I slapped him on his cut.

"Ghost, brother!" I called, and he turned bleary eyes at me. Holy fuck, he'd tied more than one on! Try like three, maybe four... Hell! I slung my backpack higher up on my shoulder and sighed.

Aaron had left me at the curb out front with a gentle squeeze of my hand. I had wanted so badly to close the gap between us, to kiss him, but he had simply smiled sadly and told me to get out of the car. I was regretting that just a little bit right now. Ghost was an sloppy drunk. He didn't need me pissed-off, though; he needed me to be supportive, and to figure out what the fuck, so I plastered a smile on my face and slipped my usual mask of 'happy' resolutely into place.

"You got my fuckin' keys?" he asked, though it took me a second to translate because it came out more like 'yougotmyfugginkeys', all mashed together.

"Yeah, man, right here, I'm here for you, brother! Let's get you home." He reeled back on his seat, and I reached out and grabbed for his shorter, more compact frame, to keep him from going off backwards.

"Have a drink with me, Squick!" he cried.

"Nawww, man! I gotta drive!" I called with a laugh. He looked at me dubiously, his hazel eyes more brown than green in the murky bar light as he squinted at me.

"I really fucked it up dinnit I?" he slurred, and despite his intoxication, his expression sobered.

"Naw, man, it's cool, I'm here," I said, not quite understanding what was up.

"Naw. She's all tore up and tattered and 'sallmyfault!" He slipped off the bar stool and stood and I grabbed onto him when he tottered. Dude was the kind of drunk that was un-freaking-real.

"C'mon, man, let me take you home." I turned to the bar, "Hey, Jimmy! He all paid up?" I asked.

"Yup! Been payin' in cash as he goes all night. Thanks for comin' to get him." Jimmy waved us off and I stooped, slinging one of Ghost's arms over my shoulders.

"Okay, buddy. Time to go home!" I led him out to the parking lot, out back, and scanned the cars and trucks a little helplessly.

"Thanks fer comin', man. You're a good kid…" He was mumbling against my shoulder.

"No problem, Ghosty, now, which one is yers?" I asked, shaking him a little.

"Tow truck," he blurted, and it was in –that way– and yep, he doubled over and heaved. I winced as the smell of vomit and whiskey wafted up from the ground and hit me full in the face. "Oh, God, that's much better!" He threw up some more. I clenched my jaw and didn't say anything, for fear that I would join him if I opened my mouth. Thankfully, he was lower to the ground than me and had good aim. He managed to miss me all together. Maybe his being a sniper had something to do with that.

"Okay, buddy, the tow truck it is. Come on." I half-walked, half-dragged him over to a black tow truck at the back of the lot. I prayed as I went through three or four keys and damned near shouted in triumph when one fit in the passenger door, and I turned the lock. Ghost was going in and out on me, and he was too heavy for me to lift on my own. I just needed to get him in the damned truck. I got the door open and helped him heave himself onto the bench seat. I slammed the door while he was still trying to right himself, careful that I wouldn't catch any of him with it. I and held my breath as I let myself into the driver's side . Thank you, Jesus! It was an automatic. I didn't know what I was going to do if it had been a standard shift. I could have driven it, but I just wasn't very good with them and I really didn't want to fuck up the dude's clutch.

I tried the key I'd used in the door in the ignition, and it wouldn't turn over. Fuck. I tried another, and another, same result.

"Come on, man!" I muttered under my breath. Ghost had like a million fucking keys on his ring.

"Is that one." He stabbed a finger at one of the keys, with a blue marker on it, and I tried it. Sure as shit, the engine turned over. I sighed.

"'K dude, where do you live?" I asked. Ghost drunkenly raised an arm and waved vaguely in a direction.

I hung my head. "Clubhouse it is. man."

At least I knew it'd be open, that there were beds, and that maybe Dragon would be there. I pulled out onto the street and drove. Ghost had his head leaned up against the passenger-side window glass and was mumbling to himself.

"She's like this flag I saw in Iraq, man... bein' pulled in the desert wind, snapping and sounding all angry, tattered, almost in shreds, but proud. You know? Because she's our flag!" He pounded his chest awkwardly at the word 'our', then his hand dropped limp into his lap. "Good 'ol U.S. of A. stars 'n bars! Tried and true," he chuckled. "Truest bluest eyes I ever seen... all my fucking fault..."

I frowned. "Dude, I have no idea what you're talking about," I said ruefully.

"Sapphire eyes!" he half-shouted and I jumped and looked at him. He blearily looked back at me and I couldn't help it. I cracked up.

"You are fuckin' lit, yo!" I laughed.

"I shoulda kilt him the first time. I didna kilt him in time..." He rested his head back against the passenger glass, and then smacked his head against it – hard. I rolled up to a stoplight and grabbed his jacket's arm and pulled him more upright to keep him from banging his head against the glass again and again.

"Dude, Ghost, you're starting to freak me out, man," and he was, his ramblings were growing darker and more morose by the second. He wasn't making sense, but at the same time his words were laced with a depth of emotion that had me sinking into a deep, foreboding dread.

"I shoulda been there, Squick. I shoulda been the one, not him." He closed his eyes and I think he passed out. I have no idea what the fuck... I drove to the clubhouse to the sound of Ghost softly snoring and pulled up into the steep drive. Dragon's and Data's bikes were out front and I breathed a bit easier. I parked the truck near the door and went into the clubhouse.

I looked up, and put my hands up, and swallowed, hard.

"The fuck you doin' here?" Dragon grated, and pointed his Browning skyward. I breathed out slowly and closed my eyes.

"Dray called me, told me to go pick up Ghost from The Spot," I said.

"Where is he?" Dragon asked, looking past me at the door, which hung open behind me.

"Passed out in the truck."

"Put yer damned hands down." Dragon waved his gun at me, grinning, and I dropped my hands to my sides and smiled.

"You scared the shit out of me," I said with a nervous laugh.

"You? What the fuck you think I was thinkin'? You've never been in an MC turf-war but I have." He cleared his throat. "Last time we had cars or trucks come by a clubhouse unexpectedly..." He didn't finish, instead, he said, "Well, never mind that. Let's go get our boy and git him to bed."

Dragon followed me out to the truck and gave a low whistle.

"Yeah, I know, right?" I said, when he went up to the passenger-side door.

"Boy got himself tore up from the floor up." Dragon tsked. "You were right to bring 'im here."

"Yeah, well, I've only been out to his place the once, for that barbeque. No fucking idea how to get out there in the dark," I told him. Dragon opened the door to the truck and Ghost slumped and fell halfway out. Dragon righted him and got under his one side, draping Ghost's arm over his broad shoulders.

"Get his other side." I moved in and got Ghost's arm up around me. He reeked like a distillery, and I grimaced. I stooped and we dragged Ghost between us, the toes of his workboots barely scraping the floor between us. It was awkward as hell for me, being so tall, but I managed.

"Where to?" I asked.

"It's a good thing we got some of these rooms finished," Dragon grunted and we went back into the sprawling complex of rooms that made up the clubhouse. It was true, we'd been working our asses off since the failed summer lake run to get the rest of the clubhouse in shape. We needed the space. Dragon and Dray had been going out on runs to try and talk some of the outlying chapters and Sacred Hearts nomads into patching over into the mother chapter to bolster our numbers.

Things remained tense with the whole Suicide Kings situation. They'd been quiet... too quiet, and Dragon called it the calm before the storm. He'd done this sort of thing before, and so he would know best, and so when he spoke, we took it to heart. It made for a darker and grimmer atmosphere and I guess I couldn't blame him for jumping at shadows. It was at this point that I felt like a total fucking moron because, like a bolt from the blue, everything that Ghost had been rambling about fell into place.

"Wonder what had his panties in such a wad," Dragon said and with a final heave we flopped Ghost onto a simply-made queen-sized bed in a sparsely-furnished spare room. I straightened and stretched.

"Shelly," I said, and Dragon cocked an eyebrow like he wasn't really surprised.

"Those two have had a thing for each other since they laid eyes on the other. Never could figure why he wouldn't tap that." He lifted a shoulder in an indelicate shrug.

"Well, come on," he said, "let's get his boots off and leave him to sleep it off." We set to work silently, letting Ghost's steel-toes hit the plain gray office-style carpet.

"Good enough," Dragon declared and we left the room. We'd left Ghost on his side, head propped on his arm. If he puked, he wouldn't drown in it. I'd still be checking on him later. This was not my first drunk-watch since becoming a prospect.

"Suppose you'll be needing a room tonight too; take the one there." Dragon indicated a room directly across the hall.

"Thanks," I said softly.

"Don't mention it, Prospect," he said, waving over his shoulder. His ponytail, long and dark, cut a black line down the middle of his tanned back to tickle the top of the equally-black butt of his gun, sticking out of his waistband.

"Hey, Dragon?" I asked, impulsively.

"Yeah, boy?" He turned and rubbed a hand over the dark whiskers on his chin, his almost-black eyes cutting back in my direction and burning a hole in my face.

"Is it really that bad?" I asked, and waved a hand to indicate the gun. He looked me over and gave a grudging nod.

"Reaver killed their President, boy. That's not something any club can, or will, let slide. No matter what thing the man done to deserve it."

I nodded and looked back in the direction of Ghost. "What do we do?" I asked.

"Well, we can't kill 'em all, so we wait. We wait to see what happens, and we hold our ground. Why, worried about yer rainbow hide?" he asked, but his eyes and smile were kind when he asked, taking any accusations of cowardice out of the question.

"No. Not mine." I answered him honestly, thinking of Aaron, of my brothers who I really did consider my family, even though I was still just a prospect. Dragon's eyes narrowed.

"He's fine for the time being. Come out here and have a drink. Seems to me you got some troubles of your own on your mind."

I nodded and followed him out to the common room. Dragon indicated a chair at a two-person table and I dropped into it. He looked me over one more time and nodded sagely.

"Think this calls for the good stuff." He went behind the bar and grabbed two glasses and a bottle from underneath and came back. He set the glasses on the table and the bottle of Jose Cuervo Reserva de la Familia between them. My eyebrows went up.

"Kid," he drawled, uncapping the bottle and pouring, "I like you."

I watched him carefully and waited for him to say more, expecting there to be a 'but'. I mean, it sounded like there was a 'but' hanging there, thick and as tangible as smoke would be curling under the low barroom lighting. Speaking of which, Dragon shook a cig out of a pack from the table and put it between his lips. He lit up and took a solid drag, holding the pack out to me. I put up a hand and shook my head politely.

When he didn't say anything I prompted him: "But..?"

He sighed, "We all got secrets, boy. We all got pasts, and we all come from somewhere, and for the most part we all accept that about one another. We don't pry unless it's required and we don't butt in where we don't belong. Take Ghost in there." He waved in the direction of the back room with the glowing end of his cig.

"Whatever is eating at him had him tie one on, but good, tonight, but you don't see us badgering him about it." He leveled a look at me, and picked up his tequila and sipped. I did the same. I wasn't usually a fan of it, but this shit was good! It went down smooth as butter.

"Yeah," I said.

"But, I bet if we asked him, he'd tell us what was what," Dragon said.

"Probably," I agreed, because that was how it was. You weren't supposed to hide things from your brothers. Guilt swirled in my chest just behind my breastbone, and the bitter taste of my lies and falsehoods choked me and turned the fine tequila I'd just drunk to ashes in my mouth. I knew what was coming. The silence hung too thick and full between us, pregnant with so many things unsaid.

"You really going to make me ask?" He sniffed and took another drag on his cigarette, jetting twin streams of smoke from his nose, so much like you would picture his namesake doing. He sighed, resigned, the silence between us having stretched for eons.

"Okay. Have it your way, boy." He stubbed out his cigarette and made to get up, and I just knew that this was it. This was the end of me and being a part of this MC, if I didn't speak up, that it was officially the end of the line, and I either put up or shrugged out of this prospect's cut here and now, and I didn't want that. I didn't want to let go of the club but terrified as I was about coming clean, I had to. It was now or never, and so I just blurted it out.

"I'm gay!"

I felt the tears rise hot and fierce, my vision blurring with them. Dragon looked at me and sank back into his seat and waited. I was waiting too, for the look of disgust, for the screaming and the yelling, for the accusations and recriminations.

"Well, it's about time," was all he said and I choked, hard. I wasn't supposed to cry! Fuck, man. Bikers didn't cry, my father's son was not supposed to be some pansy-assed faggot! And it was that last thought that had my shoulders rounding and my head bowing. The tears fell free and I fucking cried, big, wracking, shame-filled fucking tears, and waited for the first blow to land.

It landed all right, just not in the way I expected. Dragon's hand fell onto my shoulder and gripped it through the leather of my prospect's cut and jacket. He shook me back and forth gently and said, "Easy. boy. It's all right," and his voice didn't hold any malice or reproach. just a gentle, steady, rock-solid support which just made me come unglued even harder, and then Dragon, the President of the Sacred Hearts Motorcycle Club, did something completely unprecedented.

He hugged me.

5

———————

S quick...

"You all right?" he drawled after I'd settled down some. I was sitting back in my seat, numb. He pushed my unfinished glass of tequila toward me, and I stared at it for a long minute.

"Put that down," he ordered, and I obediently picked up the glass and swallowed. The alcohol burned going down my raw throat, but I welcomed it, like I welcomed the bite and sting of the needle. I sniffed.

"Been holding that in a good long while, yeah?" he asked and I nodded mutely, afraid to speak. It seemed Dragon was content to do all the talking for now.

"You're coming up, boy. You and Zander both, but that's not why you told me. I can see it plain as day. You asked me if it was really that bad with the Suicide Kings and you was thinkin' of somethin'. What was it?" he asked.

I sighed. It was out now, my dirty little secret, and I didn't know what it meant for me or for my standing with the club, but Aaron was right. I felt lighter, freer, somehow and whatever was going to happen next I didn't want to think about, but I felt like maybe I could deal with it.

"It wasn't a something, it was someone." I sucked in a breath. This wasn't something... I mean... if it were Ashton or one of the girls sitting here, this part would be a whole hell of a lot less awkward.

"Jesus Christmas, boy, just spit it out!" Dragon chuckled and I blushed.

"I met him a couple of nights ago, at the shop... he came in for a tattoo and ..." I struggled to find the words. I didn't know how to talk about this with anyone.

"Boy, I'm old... You tell my boy Dray I 'fessed up to that, I'll deny it." He lit up another cigarette. "You met a boy you thought was a hot piece of ass, am I right?"

I choked on a laugh and nodded.

"We hit it off, turned out he's um... like me."

Dragon sighed.

"Someone, I'm betting yer daddy, did a number on you, didn't he?" he asked and it was a lot kinder than I ever thought Dragon capable of.

"I, uh, I figured it out when I was around fourteen. Came out to my parents and sister when I was fifteen. My dad kicked my ass out." Dragon snorted, like he wasn't really surprised, and I winced. "Was homeless for the better part of a year when this guy, a tattoo artist named Rusty took me in."

"Did he know?" Dragon asked, and poured me a little more tequila.

"Yeah, but we never exactly talked about it." I told him what Rusty had told me and about the general don't ask/don't tell policy and Dragon shook his head with a sigh.

"You know you're going to have to come out to the rest of the guys, right? I'm not going to do it for you," he said, and I swallowed.

"Yeah, I kind of figured," I said somberly.

"You've been dealt a real shitty hand, Squick." I bowed my head.

"You know how I got that name?" I asked. Dragon arched a brow and I took it for what it was, his silent way of saying 'No, but why don't you tell me?'

"Rusty started calling me by it and I asked him why. He told me it

was because of what I was, it wasn't for him and it squicked him out."
I sighed.

"Sounds like Rusty was a pretty flawed individual," Dragon said.

"Yeah, I didn't get it. He took me in, fed me, clothed me, gave me a
job, taught me all kinds of shit and how to get by and survive. Treated
me like the kid he never had, but he always kept me at arm's length
because of what I was. He was like the father I was supposed to have
– in all things except that one area, you know?"

Dragon nodded.

"Closer than the one you were born to," he observed and I
nodded rapidly.

"By a long mile," I agreed.

"You understand that none of those people were your real family
don't you?" he asked.

"Family doesn't do that. They accept you wholeheartedly, one
hundred percent for who you are. They love you, even if they don't
always like you. They fight with you and drive you nuts like nobody's
business, but an outsider comes 'round fucking with you, then real
family is right there beside you until the outside threat is over." His
deep, dark eyes bored into my own as his words sank deep.

"The club has been like that for me. Trigger and Zander, especially, have been like that for me, I just... I'm..." I just didn't want to
see the looks of disappointment on their faces. I didn't want to see the
disgust or the shame.

Dragon leaned back in his chair and let out a gusty sigh. "You sure
you aren't sellin' 'em short?" he asked and I blinked in surprise at the
thought. I sat silent and mulled it over. He patted me on the shoulder
as he got up. "Think about it. Club meeting this Saturday night. You
can tell the rest of 'em then," he said.

"What if I can't?" I asked, quietly, needing to know.

"Can't be having secrets... of any kind. Not from your Brothers,"
he said softly, and lumbered down the back hallway.

I sat for a long time, finished my tequila and stared at my phone. I
wanted to call Aaron and, rather than fight it like I'd been fighting so
many things for so very long, I just didn't. I gave in to the urge and

dialed and felt like some kind of needy ass for doing it, but he answered on the first ring and his voice chased every doubt I'd had in my mind about calling right out of my head.

"Andy? Is your friend, I mean brother... whoever all right?" he asked me by way of greeting and I had to swallow hard past the sudden lump in my throat. Aaron seemed to get me faster than anyone I'd ever met in my entire life.

"Yeah, yeah, he's good. I had to bring him to the club, he's passed out in one of the spare rooms. I, uh, I should go check on him in a minute. I just wanted to call you," I said.

"I'm glad you did. I was a little worried, sometimes drunk people can be difficult," he said and I could hear his rueful smile.

"Yeah, well. Dragon was here, he helped me get Ghost all squared away." I paused and Aaron caught the significance behind it.

"Andy, what happened, baby?" he asked, concern shading his tone.

"Dragon and I had a talk," I said.

"–A– talk?" he asked, kindly.

"–The– talk," I affirmed solemnly. Aaron was silent for a long time.

"Oh. Um, what did he say?"

"That I was on my own for coming out to the guys, and that I'm doing it this weekend." I blew out a long breath.

"Did he seem upset?" Aaron asked.

"No."

"Disappointed?"

"No." I frowned, what was Aaron getting at?

"Dragon is your leader, yeah? The President?"

"Yeah... Aaron, what're you getting at?" I asked. I was tired from a long day at the shop and stressed-out from everything. I felt like a frayed piece of rope and my thoughts just weren't falling into line. They were just all scattered-like and so I just wasn't picking up what Aaron was putting down. I just had so much to think about... Too much to think about.

"If Dragon is your leader, and he didn't get upset, chances are pretty decent the majority fall in line with his thinking... At any rate, I'm telling you to think positive here."

"You're probably right," I hedged.

"But you're going to worry about it anyway. Tie yourself into knots?"

"Probably," I agreed, chagrined. Aaron laughed softly.

"You stuck there? Can you come back tonight?"

"I wish I could, but naw. I gotta look after Ghost." Man, I wanted very badly to curl up with Aaron and talk this out between rounds of dirty sex. He was so fucking good.

"Okay." He sounded about as disappointed as I felt.

"I gotta go," I said.

"Okay, call me tomorrow morning?"

"You bet."

We said our goodbyes, which were sappy, but surprisingly, I didn't mind so much. I hated to admit it to myself, but Aaron had become a sort of lifeline, n anchor during uncertain times and in uncharted waters for me, and I had some mixed feelings about that. On the one hand, I was so grateful that he was there and that I could talk to someone who understood... on the other hand, I was acutely aware that Aaron and I had literally just met and that doing this to him was less than fair.

I checked on Ghost, who was in rough shape. He was still dead to the world and I was glad I'd put him in the rest position because he'd gotten sick again in his passed-out state. It was going to be a long night, but one thing was for sure, I needed to have another talk with Aaron, to make sure that he was as okay as he sounded with me using him as a lifeline in all of this, because as much as I wanted to be able to stand on my own, I really had to admit to myself that I needed him. Part of me needed him behind me, in my corner. After the last couple of days of having someone beside me that knew what it was like for me, I didn't want to let that go, And, I really wasn't done getting to know him.

I liked Aaron. A lot. I guess what it really boiled down to, was that I didn't want him to feel like I was using him. I didn't want to use him.

All of these thoughts, and more, turned over in my mind as I got Ghost cleaned up and into a shower, and the bed stripped and remade. The night turned into one of the longest I ever remember living through, and when I'd been out on the street, there had been a lot of really long nights.

6

———————

S quick...

The next morning I sat at the same table in the common room that Dragon and I had used the night before. I was staring blankly into the large, steaming mug of black coffee I had cradled in my hand. I kept playing and replaying the conversation with Dragon in my head over and over again, deciding on how to best put my house in order.

I liked Aaron despite our short acquaintance, and I really wanted to give things with him a solid shot, get to know him better, spend some real time with him. I'd never felt that way about a guy before. I'd never really tried at a relationship before. All my past interludes and forays into romance could hardly be called that. Every other encounter I'd had was pretty much an anonymous encounter, or a week or two fling at best. I'd lied my ass off that first time with Aaron, telling him I didn't do one-night-stands. I just hadn't wanted to do a one-night-stand with him, because something deep down told me Aaron was different than anyone I'd met before, that Aaron deserved better, was better than that.

He was the first person I'd ever encountered that I felt an honest and true connection with., that was more than just good looks and a round of rowdy sex. Having sex with him on the first date had been impulsive as hell, sure, but there was more to it than that at the same time. Hell! I didn't know how to explain it. It just –was– and I felt so completely torn in two over it.

Now, more than ever I had before, I felt like I was at a fork in the road. Down one fork was a life with my brothers and the MC I had grown to love so dearly , and down the other, a life without hiding anymore.

I had been standing at this particular fork in the road for some time, now, with Aaron, it was more of a crossroads than just a fork. I just wasn't sure if one of the directions I could travel was an all-inclusive deal: MC, Aaron, and a life without hiding, the best of all worlds. I was chewing my lower lip and thinking about just everything, when a ragged cough brought my head snapping up.

Ghost looked like shit. His jacket and cut hung on him awkwardly, his pants were disheveled and wrinkled from sleeping in them. His hair stuck up at odd angles, greasy and unwashed. His eyes were bloodshot and bleary and he looked like he was about to keel over from exhaustion any second, but that was likely a byproduct of being hung over and of just waking up. He eyed me from across the common room warily.

"You come and get me?" he asked.

"Yup."

"Was I an asshole?" he asked and I laughed a little.

"Naw. Even when you're a depressed drunk you're a co-operative drunk," I said. He made a non-committal noise of acknowledgment and trudged into the common room, his boots chuffing against the floor with each step; he hadn't bothered to tie them or even lace them.

Ghost dropped into the seat across from me and scrubbed his face with his hands, then leaned way back in his seat, stretching. I'm pretty sure I heard his back pop a couple of times where he bent back over the backrest on the old wood chair. He let out a grunt of an exhale and sagged in the seat. I pushed my untouched cup of coffee towards him.

"Here, you need this a lot more than I do," I told him. He nodded and groped out for the mug and brought it to his face. He sucked some into his mouth and winced at the bitterness before swallowing it down.

"Dude, I feel like shit," he groused.

"Dude, you look like it, too," I shot at him, and he frowned.

"Thanks," he grated.

"You, uh, want to talk about it?" I asked. He glared at me, and stared me down until I put up my hands and ducked my head in surrender.

"Need to be anywhere?" he asked.

"Uh, yeah. I left my bike at a buddy's place. He gave me a ride to the bar so I could drive you in."

He raised his eyebrows. "You drove my work truck?" he asked.

I shrugged, "It's an automatic and it's not like you were in any shape to ride. It's fine, it's parked out front." I shook my head a little. Ungrateful bastard.

"Dude, didn't mean it like that. Don't be such a fucking queen," he said gruffly and swallowed more coffee; it was my turn to put my eyebrows up.

"Let me ask you something," I said, and I am not sure if it was my expression or my tone, but Ghost's angry expression of a second before smoothed out, his hazel eyes going a little wide.

"Sure, man..." he trailed off and slumped back in his seat from where he'd straightened with his indignance.

"Why you guys always calling me gay? Making fun of me and shit?" I asked and Ghost blinked and reddened with embarrassment.

"I... uh... er..." He exhaled harshly. "Shit, man!" he exclaimed, "I don't know... I guess it's not just any one thing. You don't give a second look to any of the club girls or ol' ladies, you sing with Ashton like it ain't no thing. When one of the girls needs an opinion on colors or whatever they go to you. I didn't think it bothered you, to be honest." He closed his mouth and looked taken aback, or surprised. I took a deep breath and soldiered on.

"What if I were? Would it make any difference?" I asked, softly, and Ghost's shoulders dropped. He looked at me, really –looked– at me, and shook his head.

"No, man. Not to me," he said softly. "Don't think Trig, or Zander, or Reave would give a fuck either. Why are you asking?" His eyes bounced in his skull as he looked me over, searching my face for any clue as to what this was all about. I chewed my lip.

"Just forget it, man. I've just got a lot on my mind," I said, and he tilted his head to the side and regarded me.

"Do –you– want to talk about it?" he asked and I stared back at him in a silent regard of my own.

When the silence had grown thick between us, he finally nodded.

"Fair enough," he said. "You ever do, you know where to find me, Brother." He held up his hand and I clasped it and shook it.

"Yeah," I nodded, "same goes for you." We sat in a comfortable silence for a time, each of us lost in our own heads, while he finished his coffee, then he drove me out to Aaron's apartment, dropping me off at the curb. He watched me go up and knock on the door and only pulled off when it opened for me and I waved down to him. Couldn't be too careful, not with the Suicide Kings yet to make a move. They were making us nervous as fuck with how quiet they'd been the last five months.

Aaron stood inside his apartment looking sleep-tousled and delicious in just a comfortable pair of pajama pants riding low on his chiseled hipbones. One tug on the draw string and he'd lose them. I eyed him hungrily and he eyed me back warily for a second. I smiled slowly and he relaxed marginally.

"You're looking at me like I'm something good to eat," he stated dryly, and I felt my smile grow.

"Don't mind if I do," I said, and pulled him against my body, picking up pretty much right where we'd been forced to leave off the night before.

S quick…

"All right, listen up!" Dragon's voice boomed through the common room and the place fell silent. It was go-time and if I'd been nervous about coming out to the club before, well now, now I was – terrified–. In addition to Dragon, Dray, Trig, Doc, Reaver, and the rest of the local Sacred Hearts mother chapter, there was something like twenty or more other guys from out-of-town, guys wearing the bottom rockers of neighboring chapters or nomad patches. I swallowed hard, my heart hammering in my chest, my mouth bone-dry as Dragon started speaking, and when Dragon spoke, you listened.

"So, we got two guys that have been prospecting for us for the last year and it's time to put 'em up for a vote, but first one of 'em would like to tell us somethin'. As most of you fuckers know, there's more to a brotherhood like ours than ridin' and fightin' and what-have-you. We're family, when a lot of us ain't got no real family to call our own. You don't hide shit from your family, and your family, they don't turn their backs on yah for anything less than the most hardcore of betrayals. So, Squick, why don't you say what you gotta say, and we'll see how this goes." Dragon crossed his bulky arms over his chest in the awkward way he had and leveled his dark gaze at me.

Leather creaked and denim rustled as everyone in the room turned to me expectantly. I felt like my friggin' heart was going to explode, but there really was no going back now. I was standing on the edge of the cliff, ready to plunge headlong into the unknown, scared as fuck about what was under the water, but it was now-or-never, it was sink-or-swim and it was time to take the plunge and so I did, the only way I knew how.

"I, uh... I didn't know what to do, I, um, I never wanted to keep this from anyone, I mean I did but..." I coughed and took a deep breath to steady myself. "I never wanted to lie to you guys, and I can't in good conscience let you guys put it to a vote, let you accept me as your brother and into this club while I hid anything, especially something this big." I hung my head and gritted my teeth. I closed my eyes for a second and took another fortifying breath, and looked Trigger and Zander in the eyes while I said it, because they had known me the longest and because they had brought me here, and because I was afraid they would catch the most hell because of that.

"I'm gay," I said. and grimaced, "and I'm sorry I've hid it for so long but... but I didn't know what else to do."

Trigger's frown smoothed into a look of relief and Zander's eyebrows went up in a look that screamed that I hadn't told him anything he wasn't aware of already. Dragon nodded and Dray's expression remained as shuttered and guarded as I had ever seen it. Our VP had a damn good poker face; I couldn't tell what he was thinking one way or the other. Reaver was grinning like he'd won the lottery; I didn't know if that was a good or a bad thing and I shivered inside. After watching him last Lake Run, coming up the cabin trail in the dark with his hands caked in blood, his shorts smeared with it and straining over his boner... Well, I liked my mentor, I really did, but I really didn't want to find out what his apparent glee at the situation meant, especially if it didn't mean anything good.

"Okay." Dragon sucked his teeth and looked out over everyone in attendance, "Let's put it to a vote." He looked at me. "Has to be unanimous, you understand," he said, and I nodded.

"All in favor?" Dray called and put up his hand and I felt my chest crush down with emotion. It looked like every hand in the house went in the air. Dragon nodded.

"All opposed?" Dray asked and all the hands dropped, but two went up. My heart dropped into my stomach and my shoulders with it. I felt cold all over and I closed my eyes. Two hold-outs did not unanimous make. Never mind that they were out-of-towners, they were still patched members of this club and their votes counted. At least, I think they did.

"That's fucking BULLSHIT, man!" We all startled and turned to Zander who was seething next to Trigger. All eyes were rooted to the stocky man who was just getting warmed up.

"Man, fuck you two!" he shouted, pointing in their direction. "You've been here what? A couple of days? Well Squick's been here for over a fucking year, you asswipes! Pouring his blood, sweat, and tears into this fucking club! You cut that skinny fucker and he bleeds Sacred Hearts colors!"

Zander rounded on our cabinet.

"You really going to let these two fucks influence this decision?" he demanded. Dray opened his mouth to speak and it looked bad, it looked really bad.

"Man, fuck you! You fucking fucks! Squick is my brother! My fucking family and I don't turn my fucking back on my fucking family!"

He took a breath to rail on but was stopped short by Dragon's booming laughter. We turned to the President of the chapter in a bit of stunned confusion as he just fucking howled with laughter.

"What's so fucking funny, old man?" Zander demanded, still fucking –heated–.

"Boy!" Dragon cried at Zander, "look at them two!" Zander looked back at the two hold-outs, who were both grinning. Zander's face collapsed into a hard scowl.

These guys aren't from our chapter and don't get a say. We done already fucking voted on you two!"

Dragon howled, and Zander and I exchanged looks. Dray was grinning now, too, and so was everyone else.

"Squick, c'mere," Dragon said and crooked a finger at me, still laughing. I went numbly to our president's side. He put his arm around my shoulders and I startled.

"Boy, we all talked about it a month or more ago and decided you were in as long as you would come clean about who you were. Took you a minute, but you finally got there. You do you, and the you we know is loyal to a fault, has always been there for a brother no matter what time of night no matter what the fucking issue. You are a damned fine asset to this club and we would've been damned sorry to see you go, but we all knew you wouldn't let that happen, that we could count on you and sure enough! So that left Zander. You know we can't resist fucking with you guys, and I can't say we're sorry we fucked with him at your expense."

I blinked, stunned... "What are you saying?" I asked, my words hollow in my chest.

"I'm saying," he said, gripping me by the shoulders and turning me towards Reaver who held a brand new Sacred Hearts cut in his hands, "welcome, brother Disney."

Dragon gave me a little shove in Reaver's direction, taking the prospect's cut off my shoulders when he did it. I stepped forward, shaking, and turned around so Reaver could slide the new cut onto my shoulders.

"Disney?" I asked, wonderingly.

"On account of all them fucked-up cartoons you got all over you," Dragon said, grinning. I looked over to Trigger, who wore a shit-eating grin, and to Zander, who looked as stunned as me.

"Zander," Dray said, and Zander looked over to his mentor, our VP, who was shaking out another, larger cut.

"Not anymore," Dragon said. "Revelator, on account of getting hit by you is one, a revelation, that is. You've proven in the last year that no matter how bad it gets, no matter how sideways shit goes that you've got any man in this club's back. You've gone above and beyond and done what needs done to serve this club, protect this club and its people, and we couldn't ask for two better brothers than you and Disney." Zander shuffled forward on his red Chuck Taylor's. He shrugged out of his prospect's cut and let Dray help him into his new colors, and looked about as overcome by emotion as I felt.

"Congratu-fucking-lations you two," Dragon said, then roared like his namesake, "Welcome home!" The room erupted in loud cheering and applause punctuated by earsplitting whistles of approval. Hugs were handed out like cigars at a baby shower and by the time it was over, my ribs felt loose and my back bruised, from all the sound poundings they'd taken.

"Disney," I said under my breath, finger tips smoothing across the ridge of embroidery of my new road name. I felt my face split into a smile. I liked it. I liked my new name a lot. Then I swallowed hard and sobered.

"Uh oh, what's that look for?" Reaver asked. I looked up at him, Zan- Revelator, Trigger, my Pres. and Vice Pres.

"Is it okay... I mean, is it going to be weird if..." They all looked at me like they weren't getting it. Ghost shouldered his way between Trig and Revelator with three beers in each hand, holding the bottle necks between his fingers.

"Spit it out, Disney," Trig said, amused.

"Is it going to be weird for you guys if I bring my boyfriend around?" I rushed out, thinking of Aaron. The guys all exchanged looks, and some of them had the grace to look embarrassed by their discomfort, but it was Dray of all people who spoke up first...

"Dis, man, I'm not going to pretend that it isn't going to make me uncomfortable at first, but that's my malfunction, not yours. I'll get used to it the more I see it," he said and gave me a nod.

"Not sure how we're going to handle it, I mean, does he have any interest in prospecting? Is he going to be your Old Lady? We're forging new ground here, the club has never had a gay member, so we're all on a learning curve with you, boy," Doc said.

"Um, I don't know either, Aaron and I have only been seeing each other for about a week, it, uh, it was all real sudden and real new... I'm, uh..." I blushed. I wasn't used to being so open about all this.

"Where's he at?" Zander asked, his eyes narrowed.

"He plays the cello for the Philharmonic Orchestra in the city," I said.

Ghost put the beers on the bar when Dragon started looking from one to another of his chapter.

"It's a clear night. Why don't we just go get 'im and find out?" Dragon asked.

I startled.

"I... don't know!" I said, drawing out the 'I'.

"Ashamed of us, Puddin'?" Revelator asked, wrinkling his nose and smiling a toothy grin. I gave him a flat look.

"Fuck you, let's go, but you guys have to let me talk to him first!" I cried, and they all started getting rowdy and cheering.

Oh God... how was this going to go?

8

S^{quick} Disney...

We rode out in formation, the guys from out-of-town staying back at the club-house to hold down the fort until we got back. Reaver had called his wife and told her to get the girls together and their pretty little asses to the clubhouse if they wanted to meet my boyfriend, and had to hold the phone a foot from his ear as her and Ashton's ear-splitting squeals of delight had blasted through the earpiece.

"I hate you so goddamned much," I said in a dry, deadpan tone of voice but I couldn't keep the smile off my face. He sucked in his cheeks and gave me fish lips and made smooching sounds in my direction, and I flipped him the fucking bird.

Dragon came to me and handed me a pillion pad for my back fender. I smiled and took it and pressed the seat's lick-and-stick suction cups to my back fender and I really, really hoped that it would get used.

Adrenaline coursed through my veins, thrumming with a low hum through every nerve ending. A mixture of excitement and anxiety played the insides of my ribs like a xylophone, my heart hammering a bass beat against the underside of my breastbone, the closer we got to the city.

The night was clear and the sky, which was shot through with stars over the clubhouse, was merely sprinkled with them the closer and closer we got to the lights of the city. It was almost an hour's ride and it honored me that my brothers would take it with me. We pulled up to the taxi waiting area along the curb in front of the Orchestra House and waited. I checked the time and the timing couldn't be more perfect. The performance had ended a half hour ago and the musicians were just coming out the side door. I blew into my icy hands to warm them, looking back at the guys, who all sat astride their bikes and waited.

"Well, go get him!" Trigger barked, and laughed. I shot a grin over my shoulder and walked towards the mouth of the alley where the performers were coming out a side door and watched for Aaron. My heart nearly stopped in my chest when he came out. He was between a girl who carried a slim case for a clarinet or a flute and a guy who carried a violin. Aaron's cello was in a soft case that he wore like a backpack and he looked up sharply at the girl's startled "Oh, my!"

His liquid dark eyes locked with mine and all the tension I'd felt on the way out here eased marginally. I held out my hands to either side and laughed a little helplessly. Aaron blinked behind his sexy-as-hell lenses and looked past me to the gleaming line of chrome and dusky black leather at the curb.

"Andy," he asked, "what's going on?"

"Well, uh, my brothers thought it might be a good idea if we came out and picked up my boyfriend so he could celebrate me patching in with me," I said, and pursed my lips. My heart was fucking hammering in my chest as I waited for Aaron to say something.

"Oh... well, um," he smiled softly and his eyes glinted with mischief. "What's your boyfriend's name? I'll tell him you're here," I stepped closer slowly, and shrugged my shoulders nonchalantly.

"You, uh, really want to play this game, huh?" I asked, and put a smile on my face that would make Reaver proud. Aaron gasped and I smiled a little bigger, and before he or his friends could react, shot out my hand, hooking it around the back of his neck and pulling his face to mine in a fierce kiss. Aaron smiled against my mouth and kissed me back, and any fear or apprehension I had been feeling about coming here evaporated.

The girl gasped and his male friend said "Damn!" like he was impressed, and meanwhile my guys cheered and hollered from back at the bikes. Some clapping and an odd whistle or two split the city air and Aaron pulled back from the kiss.

"Um, guys, I'm going to have to catch you later, my boyfriend's come to give me a ride home. Drinks next week?" he asked.

"Absolutely," the girl said, smiling.

"Thanks, Anya," Aaron said and nodded to the dude, "Mark."

"No problem, man," Mark said, smiling. "I'm happy for you." He linked arms with Anya and they went up the alley and turned down the block.

"Glad I carpool with Anya," he said, his breath frosting the air. I smiled.

"Come and meet the guys? The girls are waiting for us back at the club house." He nodded and we went toward the line of bikes, hand-in-hand.

"Hey!" Trigger called as we got near, "Disney's told us nothin' about you!" He used the tone reserved for meeting someone and saying 'Oh so-and-so has told us so much about you!' and then the bastard gave us a shit-eating grin. Aaron tripped on a laugh and winked.

"Well, he's told me enough about you to tell me you're Trigger, and that you must be Reaver," he said, turning to my mentor. "And Zander, and Dragon, and Dray," he said, turning to each of them in turn. "I'm assuming you're Doc, and that makes you, Ghost, and you, Data," he finished. Everybody smiled broadly as he recognized them from their descriptions.

"Gypsy would have been here but it's cold, and dude is getting older, so his joints don't much like ridin' in it. It's nice to meetcha." Dragon said, and held out a meaty hand to shake.

"Hey!" Revelator called from down the line. "I'm freezing my balls off and I want a beer, can we get this show on the road?" Aaron laughed and I took him over to my bike. Reaver held out a spare helmet to me on the way by, and I gave him a grateful look. Aaron was in a peacoat and had traded his fancy duds for jeans and Converse inside, before he'd come out. I went through what I needed him to do for me as a passenger. He listened and once I had my bike kicked to life, got on behind me.

"You should call her Devi!" Aaron called over my shoulder and I looked back at him and smiled. He was talking about a female character from the Johnny the Homicidal Maniac comic books, the only one to ever get away from Nny.

"The one who got away?" I called back over the roar of more bikes starting up.

"The one who lived!" Aaron called back and I laughed.

"Put your hands in my pockets if they get cold and hang on!" I yelled and fell into my place among the pack of motorcycles pulling out. This was easily the best night of my life. Hands down.

Disney...

It was quiet and dark and about a week after me becoming a fully-patched member of the Sacred Hearts. I lay in Aaron's bed, his head on my chest, listening to him breathe, and felt contentment swallow me whole. Life was good. Really good. The club was doing well adjusting to having me and Aaron together and there were only a few looks of discomfort and only one of the out-of-town members had left stating he couldn't handle watching two dudes hold hands. As soon as the door had shut behind him Dragon had turned to Data who wordlessly had gone for his media room.

I almost felt bad for the dude, likely a call was placed to his home chapter and when the order came from the national president? Well, it got followed. The dude was gone the same day. No one around here seemed fazed by the dude leaving and no one had spoken on it since. He was just gone.

Aaron and I hadn't changed a goddamned thing about how affectionate we were with each other. If anything, the more comfortable we grew with the guys and the more comfortable they grew with us, the more Aaron and I sharing a kiss or a swat on the ass seemed to be commonplace.

Ashton and the rest of the women had immediately adopted Aaron as one of the Old Ladies. Some conversations had taken place and some ground rules had been established, and I think once that had happened and some of the mystery had been taken out of things, things seemed to dovetail with one another nicely.

It had been agreed upon that Aaron was firmly in with the Old Ladies and was, for all intents and purposes, the girl of the relationship when it came to the club and club business. We decided we'd worry about the finer points in how we interacted with other clubs later. While we could give a fuck about what the Suicide Kings thought, we weren't entirely sure how to go about things when it came to getting together with other outfits. For the most part this was okay. My relationship status was breaking new ground for the club and we were kind of the pioneers on how this would work. Playing it by ear was just how it was going to be and we were all okay with that for now.

"What are you thinking about?" Aaron asked quietly and I startled a bit I thought he had been asleep.

"Just about how we're forging new ground as a club, but mostly about how amazing you're being, putting up with all of this while we figure out how things work," I told him. He shifted and turned onto his stomach, resting an arm across my chest, his chin on his arm. He peered at me through the deep gloom of the fall night and I smiled, knowing damned well he couldn't really see me for shit without his glasses. I reached out to the side table where they rested and plucked them off the tabletop and slid them onto his face for him. His lips curled into a little appreciative smile and, not for the first time, I was struck by just how damned beautiful he was.

"Andy..." he started, then let out a breath, searching for where to start. I raised my eyebrows, amused, and smiled patiently, waiting for him to continue. "I first saw you and I thought, 'Wow, this guy isn't afraid of what people think of him!'" He swallowed. "I didn't realize how all the colors and images were a diversionary tactic, that you were making it so people wouldn't look too closely." I blinked; I'd never thought of it that way before but what he said made sense.

"I never thought of it that way before," I said honestly, speaking my thoughts.

"When I saw you it was instant attraction and the more I get to know you, the more, I don't know, content? No, the happier I am. We're like two peas in a pod it feels like." He smiled and I felt my lips curve as I watched his.

"I'm comfortable with you too, you came at just the right time and changed everything for the better, and I can't tell you–" I was interrupted by my phone vibrating across the bedside table. We both looked at it, and with a little sigh of impatience, I picked it up. It was Revelator and there was no telling what he was calling for, so with a gusty sigh, I raised my eyebrows at Aaron. He smiled a little broader and told me to answer it, so I did.

"Hello?"

"You near the shop?" Rev asked, by way of greeting, and he sounded fucking irritated. I knew the feeling.

"I'm at Aaron's, so yeah, why?" I asked.

"Fucking alarm, go check it out?" he asked. I felt my frown ease and glanced at Aaron who was already moving off of me.

"Yeah," I grunted. I couldn't bitch; he had checked it out the last couple of times.

"Thanks, kid." He hung up.

"Wonder what crawled up his ass and died," I mused aloud. Aaron shrugged. I pulled on my discarded leather pants and the black button-down shirt, doing it up right quick. I'd taken Aaron on a ride after I'd gotten off work and we'd dressed for the road and for the chill, but also to look nice enough if we'd decided to go out to dinner or stop at a club which, yeah, hadn't happened. We'd come straight back here for another rousing round of extremely hot sex.

Aaron held out my jacket and cut and I shrugged into them and zipped up, pulling on my gloves. He held out my helmet, and leaned in for a kiss like some dutiful housewife. We hadn't even needed to speak. I marveled at him, not for the first time, and kissed him fiercely.

"Hurry home, I've been sleeping better with you in my bed than without," he said gently. I gave him a crooked grin.

"Should only be twenty minutes, tops. I go, clear the alarm, call the company and bitch, and come back," I kissed him one more time, quickly, and plucked the helmet from his long-fingered hands. He closed the door behind me against the pervasive autumn chill and I huffed out a breath, watching it plume in the damp night air.

It'd been raining, the ground had that slick wet sheen from it, and the clouds still hung overhead but thankfully, the rain had stopped falling, so I wouldn't get soaked. Aaron and I had made it back to his place just as the first fat drops of rain had started to pelt us; we'd stashed my bike underneath the stairwell. I put my weight behind pulling her out now. I rolled her down the short cement walkway and out from under the apartment building's eaves onto the glimmering blacktop of the back parking lot.

It was a short ride to the shop, and I had a sinking feeling in my chest the moment I pulled up into the lot. The alarm was blaring loudly into the night, too loudly, because the front window to the shop had a gaping hole in it, the glass ragged and angry where a brick or something had been thrown through it. I stopped my bike and got off, pulling my cell from my pocket. I turned my back on the shop and plugged my opposite ear with my gloved finger while the call rang through to Zander.

"Yeah?" he asked.

"Hey boss, it's something this time. The front window's been busted out and..." I didn't get to finish my sentence. The world erupted into a cacophony of light and I was thrown forward onto my face. The lip of my German-style helmet connected with the gritty asphalt a fraction of a second before my cheek did. My hand spasmed around the phone in a crushing grip as I felt my face slide forward across the rough ground. I couldn't hear, I couldn't really see; my vision was blurred, and I had no fucking idea what had just happened.

I lay there on my stomach, stunned, my face scraped raw on the ground, a burning sensation in the back of my right thigh. I tried to drag some air into my lungs, the breath knocked clean out of me. I think the rain had started to fall again. Big fat drops with real substance pelted the back of my jacket and cut. The heel of my left hand burned from a raw scrape but my wrist, my wrist was a deep, sharp, grinding pain that made me gasp.

My hearing came back in stages, my sight recovering much faster. I tried to push myself up, but I was just so disoriented. Bits of paper and charred wood and things were pelting the ground around me. I blinked, confused, as one of the burning pieces of paper landed inches from my nose. I blinked again, trying to focus. A playing card, the edges blackening and curling, flame licking along the image of the King of Hearts –the Suicide King. I groaned and shook my head and tried to drag myself to my feet again. I could hear sirens in the distance, and the steady, even thump of my heart.

No. Not my heart. The steady, even thump of booted feet, growing closer.

I turned my head and blinked at a pair of black motorcycle boots and frayed light denim before one of the feet drew back and flew forward. I threw my arms in front of my face just in time, the kick skidded off my forearm, the one I'd hurt in my fall. Agony licked through my wrist and the boot glanced off my helmet. The sound of a fire truck's horn split the acrid night air and the booted feet took off running, spooked by how close it sounded. I blinked at the retreating image of the Suicide Kings colors, and suddenly Aaron was there, shouting, running across the parking lot at me, the lenses of his glasses alight with the raging fire behind me, consuming Open Road Ink, and my livelihood with it.

I let my eyes close as fire fighters and police moved in; I wouldn't open them again until I was in the back of the ambulance and we were moving, Aaron's hand clutching my uninjured one. I didn't want to see him hurt and I didn't want to watch it burn.

I felt sick.

Disney...

The Suicide Kings had blown up Open Road Ink. It still seemed so surreal, like something that didn't happen in real life. This is something you saw on TV, not something that happened in the really-real world, but watching TV didn't hurt like my wrist or the back of my leg. It didn't have the people you loved most crowded around your hospital bed, looking at you with expressions of grave concern.

"All right, all right, give him some room!" Doc said good-naturedly. Everyone except Aaron and Ashton moved off. Aaron held my good hand while Ashton's small hand petted up and down my shoulder under the hospital gown. Brightly colored patches of my skin winked through the openings where the shoulders of the white and light blue open-assed monstrosity snapped together.

"Am I good to talk?" Doc asked, waving generally in the direction of the club members crowding my little ER alcove. Zander, Trig, Reaver, Ghost, and Dragon were all here. Hayden had done her best to drag the rest of the crew off for hospital cafeteria coffee or vending machine coffee, much to Everett's protestations. She'd finally declared loudly that she'd go with them, but wouldn't be drinking any of that shite, in her fine Irish accent.

I nodded at Doc to let him know it was okay, absolving him of any HIPPA violation sins and he nodded and let out a pent-up breath.

"You are one lucky son of a bitch, Disney," he said without preamble. "Your wrist is busted, but not too bad; you needed some stiches in the back of your leg from a chunk of flying glass;" he held up a baggie with a wicked sharp piece of broken glass in it, stained with my blood and his lips compressed in a thin line, "and if you hadn't had your helmet on and been wearing all that leather you'd pretty likely be burned. It was a good thing you had your back to the blast too." He shook his head and let out a gusty sigh.

"Didn't see this coming," Trigger remarked and it was as if his words bore the weight of the world in regret, "Should've, but didn't."

"When they didn't find any bastard dealings on our part they went for the legitimate ones," Dragon grunted.

Aaron's fingers tightened around my own.

"Are these people trying to kill you?" Aaron asked me, his deep, dark eyes drilling into my own. Several of us startled; some of my brothers traded guilty looks. Ashton reached across me and put her hand over Aaron's. He startled in turn, and looked at her.

"It's not always like this," she murmured. "Some things happened, one of them hurt one of us, we tried to forge a friendship from the tragedy, then over the summer we invited them to join us on an outing and they hurt one of us again... badly. We couldn't be nice a second time." Her golden eyes were at once sad and burning bright with a ferocity I'd never seen in her. She looked to Trigger and Reaver and something passed between the three of them. Aaron swallowed.

"What am I missing?" he asked. Dragon cleared his throat.

"That's club business, son," our president said, and Aaron nodded, his eyes seeking out my own.

"What happens now?" he asked, and he was a little too pale for my tastes.

"That's club business too," Reaver said solemnly, and Doc sighed, resigned.

"I've said it before and I'll say it again, I'm getting too old for this." He shook his head, "Church?" he asked Dragon.

"As soon as you can get to the house."

"Off in three hours."

"That'll do," Dragon said and Doc nodded.

"I'll get your discharge paperwork started. Concussion-watch, he has one," Doc said to Trig and Zander, who grinned. Zander... shit, I mean Revelator, Rev... the name changes were happening quicker than heat lightning lately and I was having trouble keeping up. Anyway, Rev sometimes took on fights in his spare time. Underground MMA shit, for fun, to make a little money on the side, but mostly as a way of blowing off steam. As a result, he'd had more than a few concussions he'd needed babysitting through, and I'd been the babysitter. Guess it was time for him to return the favor. Aaron squeezed my hand again and I looked up.

"You're staying with me... right?" he asked . Dragon answered for me.

"Naw, I think it's best if all of y'all come to the clubhouse. You too, lover boy. Leastways until we get some things figured." Aaron chewed his lower lip and nodded finally.

I frowned.

"How did you get to the shop?" I asked him.

"I heard the explosion, I threw on some sweats and I ran... I don't know how I knew, I just did. I just knew it was you." His face crumbled into lines of confusion, fear, and concern and I pulled on the front of his sweater, bringing his lips down to mine. He was in his pajamas, feet stuffed into Converse without the benefit of socks, his plaid pajama pants in blues and greens clashing with the burnt-orange sweater he'd been wearing earlier on in the day. His lips moved carefully across my own and I sighed. He rested his forehead against mine and I had no way of telling him that I had been just as scared as he was of losing what we had going on between us when it was still so fragile and so new, of how afraid I was that I could and would still lose it. I didn't think Aaron was handling this too well, and that scared me. It scared me more than when I was laying on the blacktop outside the shop, with pieces of building raining down around me.

"Just please don't go," I whispered. "Not yet,"

Aaron drew back startled.

"I'm not going to." His voice was gentle and held some finality. I nodded, mute for the moment, afraid my voice would betray me. I didn't think I could keep it steady. Plans were being made around us for transportation and the like, who would be riding with who, and that sort of thing. Ashton offered to take Aaron home for some clothes and things but he simply pursed his lips and shook his head, his hand tightening around mine.

I closed my eyes and tried to rest a little bit. Doc brought me some blue hospital scrub pants that were, of course, too short in the legs for me but they covered my ass and that was a marked improvement, in my opinion. They'd cut my pants off to get at the back of my leg. Doc wouldn't let them cut my jacket and cut. Those were more than a little worse for wear. The patches on the back of my cut were singed bad and the leather around them pitted and torn from flying glass. The double layer of the leather vest and the leather of my jacket had stopped it from reaching my skin; the single layer of leather of the pants on my legs had done the job, except for the bigger piece of glass. I had some cuts and scratches on the back of my neck where there was a gap between my helmet and collar, but they weren't too bad. The scrape on my cheekbone stung like a son of a bitch but Doc had smeared some pain-relieving antibiotic ointment on it after a nurse had cleaned it.

Aaron helped me pull my jacket and cut on over my bare chest and I leaned on him, my arm around his shoulders as they transferred me into a wheelchair for the trip to the lobby. I wanted to protest the chair, but I felt like I'd been hit by a truck, so I didn't. Maybe I should have, with how many looks of concern it earned me. Aaron and I would be riding with Trig and Ashton to the club. I may have drowsed some, leaning against Aaron in the back seat because the trip felt really, really short.

Too soon, Trig was pulling open the back door and I was leaning heavily on both him and Aaron as we made our way into the club and down the corridor to the room that had been designated as mine. I think I was asleep before they even laid me down on the king-sized bed, which was little more than a mattress and box spring stacked in the middle of the floor.

11

Disney...

I was shaken awake by Aaron, laying on one side of me, and a kneeling Rev on the other, a glass of water thrust into my hand.

"Hey, Puddin'! Drink up, man, you gotta stay hydrated." I blinked blearily at Rev and brought the glass to my lips, greedily drinking it down in great draughts. I glared at Rev over the glass while I did it. He'd been mockingly calling me 'Puddin'' for years and it still grated on my nerves every time he did it. He grinned at me impishly. Damn bastard knew it, too.

"What time is it?" I asked.

"A little after three," Aaron answered softly and I winced. Judging by the dark and the electric perimeter light shining through the room's high window, it was three in the morning, not the afternoon, which meant I hadn't slept as much as I had hoped.

"Concussion-watch, remember?" Rev gave me a look like he was trying to discern something by my response.

"I got blown up. I'm tired and I just want sleep..." I said grouchily, which was only partially the truth. I wanted sleep, and I wanted Aaron. I looked him over, his dark eyes glittering in the close dark and I handed the empty glass to Rev. I laid my head on Aaron's shoulder, turning my back on my boss and friend, and held my boyfriend close.

"Yeah. I get you," Rev said and stood and I could hear the smile in his voice. "People in Hell want ice water too, though Squi-Disney. I'll be back to wake you up again in an hour and then you're going to have to get your ass up. We got Church." He left the room and shut the door behind him and I was suddenly, and gratefully, alone with Aaron.

"Hey," I said, listening to the steady thrum of his heartbeat through his trim chest.

"Hey," he said back, his long hands smoothing over my naked back. I was warm, almost too warm from sleep and the comforter we had thrown over us. It was a bit stuffy in the room but I didn't care. All I cared about right now was that Aaron was here with me and that he was holding me. The weight of things unspoken, questions unasked, was heavy on both of us, a silent, crushing weight.

"What –can– you tell me?" he asked quietly and I could hear the distress in his voice. I sighed. I was torn. I wanted to tell him everything, keep no secrets. I was sure that the guys told their women more than they were supposed to. I mean shit, Irish wouldn't take anything less fromof Dray than the total truth, but then again, she knew better than to speak of it to anyone else. I worried the ring in my lip with my tongue and sighed. I guess it really boiled down to if I could trust Aaron or not and truth was... truth was, this was all so damned new! I'd never had anything like this before in my life and I wanted so badly to be able to tell him everything but my past encounters dictated that trusting anyone was just pure fucking idiocy. Trust had to be earned and that took time, but it was a two-way street, too, and so I decided to give a little. Just a little. The trick was telling him what was common knowledge; what he'd learn within a few weeks of him being here anyway.

"About a year ago, Everett was working this coffee stand. The early morning shift. Dray had just dropped her off and this guy walks up to the window and sticks a gun in her face. Starts screaming at her to open the safe. Problem was, she didn't have the combination. Only her boss did." Aaron was utterly silent, eyes locked on mine in the dark, listening with rapt attention.

"Everett told him but he wasn't hearing any of it and so he shot her, in the leg. She was lucky, he was only packing a .22, so it didn't permanently damage anything, but still, he shot her. Dray had gone back for something. I don't know what, they don't talk about that part, but anyways, he pulls up just as the douchebag pulls the trigger and Dray, he went apeshit on the guy and beat the fuck out of him. The kid was one of the Suicide Kings, this biker gang that set up shop just across the county line."

Aaron's eyes went wide. "What happened?" he asked.

"Dragon and Dray, they brokered a deal with the President and Vice President of the Suicide Kings. The Sacred Hearts are good guys, upstanding guys, but they weren't always. Long before I joined they were into heavy shit, drug- and money-running, but not anymore. They haven't been for a long time, but they still have that reputation and they used it to broker a deal with the Suicide Kings. If they threw the kid that shot Evy out of their club, the Sacred Hearts would shake hands with the Suicide Kings and all would be forgiven; they didn't,then the Sacred Hearts and Suicide Kings were officially at war."

Aaron swallowed hard, "I thought Ashton said you guys had been friends," he observed.

"Yeah they threw the kid out. Shot him in the leg with a .38 and declared him out bad, that's out of the club on bad terms which means he comes across one of them he's likely to get his ass beat. True to our word the Sacred Hearts declared satisfaction and even did some joint rallies and events with the Suicide Kings. As soon as spring hit, we did a charity ride with them and raised something like eighteen grand for the Wounded Warrior Project. We invited them to join us on our Summer Lake Run which we held early this year. Usually we do it Labor Day weekend but this year in recognition for our success with the fundraiser we did it Fourth of July weekend."

Aaron looked thoughtful, his hands smoothing up and down my back and arms in aimless patterns with no rhyme or reason to them. I closed my eyes and lost myself in the sensation for a minute and must have started to drift back to sleep, because his hands stopped and he shook me lightly.

"What happened, Andy?" he asked me. I let out a huge sigh.

"It was us, the Suicide Kings and this outfit from down in Florida that Reaver and Hayden had met when Reaver took Hayden on her honeymoon." Aaron frowned and I grinned, "She got dumped at the alter by her douchebag ex, they didn't get married 'til last month." Aaron's eyes got wide.

"Oh, this I have to hear, but not right now. Who were they?" he asked. I nodded. He had a lot to catch up on if he were going to hang with this crowd, but not all of it was my story to tell.

"The 'they' you're asking about being the crew from Florida?" I asked just to be sure. He nodded.

"They're an MC known as the Kraken. It was a good thing too, we never would have been able to handle what went down without their numbers backing ours. The Suicide Kings have about three or four times our numbers, or did, before Dragon and Dray started recruiting," I explained. Aaron's eyes widened.

"What happened that was so bad that you were willing to take on those kinds of odds?" he asked and I smiled to myself. I loved that he was so smart.

"Shelly happened," I said, somberly.

"What did they do?" he asked dubiously. He'd met Shelly, or rather the version of who she was now. Shelly used to be this spitfire, a total firecracker who lived free, didn't take shit from anyone, and was forever laughing and causing some kind of mischief. Now she was sullen, angry, sad, and irritable on a good day, and lashing out and a total bitch on a bad one. There had been a lot more bad days than good lately.

"The President of the Suicide Kings took her, hauled her out into the woods and..." I didn't like saying it out loud. Saying it out loud made it real, made it ugly, and made me and just about every other guy in the club feel guilty and dirty as Hell for not protecting her better. For not looking out for her.

"He raped her?" Aaron asked quietly.

"And knocked the shit out of her," I affirmed.

"What did you do?" he asked me. I pursed my lips.

"I did what my President told me to do. I stayed at the cabin and watched over the girls while he and the rest of my brothers handled it." I took a deep breath and let it out slowly.

"And that's why they're mad?" he asked quietly.

"Yeah," my voice was soft while I said it, and I prayed Aaron wouldn't make me elaborate further.

"He hurt her, you guys beat him up I don't understand..." I made a frustrated noise and sat up. I cupped Aaron's face in my hands.

"I can't talk about what was or was not done, baby, but please understand me when I say that Shelly is Reaver's cousin." I stared into his eyes and willed him to get it, but Aaron didn't have that street-smart self-preserving instinct like so many of us had. Aaron had a good life, with loving parents and good schools and the kind of upbringing the rest of us had only dreamed of or thought was made for TV. He just blinked at me, confusion clouding his liquid dark eyes, and I suddenly felt hopeless and all wrong for him. I closed my eyes and felt a wave of defeat come over me.

"I don't understand." he searched my face, his crumpled into lines of confusion, "Reaver is a nice guy, a happy-go-lucky kind of dude. I feel really bad about what happened to his cousin; Shelly is a pretty girl from what I can tell. What am I missing?" he asked. I sighed.

"I think I've said all I can, for now," I chewed my bottom lip. Aaron swallowed and nodded, but he didn't look happy.

"The less I know, the better?" he asked, and I nodded solemnly.

"Yeah. That about covers it." I held his hands in mine in our laps.

"I don't know, Andy... You tell me your club is just a club that they don't do anything illegal and everything is above-board but you guys clearly did something bad because you won't talk about it. I mean what could be worse than–" he stopped and his dark eyes widened, as he finally got it, I think.

"Shhh, don't say anything," I put my fingertips to his lips and he looked at me like he was seeing me for the first time ever.

"What did you do?" he asked, and the question was full of fear and horror.

"Aaron, I swear to you, I did exactly what I told you. I sat on the front porch of that cabin and watched out for the girls inside. I didn't hurt anybody, I didn't even have to threaten anybody. The guys went out, handled what needed handling and left me with the order to shoot anything that wasn't in Sacred Hearts or Kraken colors. I didn't have to though, no one that wasn't supposed to be there came around. It was just me and the girls."

Aaron gave me a hard look.

"Would you have?" he asked, bluntly.

"Would I have, what?" I asked.

"Shot one of them if they came around... done what they told you to do?" He was looking at me as if the answer to this question would decide a lot of things, and I felt totally alone. I took my hands from his and fixed my gaze on a stray goose feather on top of the comforter.

"If it came down to it, and they were coming to hurt one of the girls or cause trouble at the cabin, yes. I would have done everything to warn them off first, but if they were coming to hurt Ashton or Everett or Shelly, or any of them, I would have protected my own. This is my family, Aaron." I sniffed and felt my shoulders drop as he scooted off the bed.

"I'm not a violent guy, Andy," he said.

"I'm not either, Aaron, you gotta believe that, but I didn't start this. None of us did, and I can't –and won't– let those animals hurt these people. Or me, or you. I love this club and the people in it. At the end of the day, these guys, these women, they're all I've got in the world. I have no more mother, no more father or sister. They turned their backs on me, but you know what? These guys never will. Never. Not ever, and I won't turn my back, either." I was getting angry. I knew it wasn't at Aaron, it was just 'angry' seemed like such a better option right now than 'hurt' and Aaron was fixing to hurt me but good. I'd let him get under my skin, let him in far too quickly, and I was about to pay the price.

Stupid. Stupid. Stupid.

"I need to think about all of this," he said, quietly. I nodded, mutely. I didn't trust myself to speak. The silence stretched between us. Finally I broke it, and it killed me to do it.

"I'll have Sunshine or Doll drive you home. Thanks for coming to the shop, for being at the hospital." I got up a little too quickly and swayed on my feet. Aaron reached out but I took a step back. I didn't want to add to an already shitty-enough night. Clean break, like ripping off a Band-Aid; that was the best way to go with these kinds of things, right?

"Please, don't do that, please, no, I don't quite know what to do with all of this, Andy, this is a lot... You almost died! You got blown up! And now you're telling me you're in the middle of some kind of war with a rival motorcycle gang and that people have been getting shot and raped and, and, and... disappeared? It's a lot to process and I don't know what to do or how to deal, and so I just need a little bit of time to think!" he looked like he was about to cry and I listened to everything he was saying, and even though it fucking hurt like a son of a bitch, he was right.

I was ass-deep in trouble and sinking fast, and it had the potential to bleed all over him, and I didn't want that. I didn't want him getting hurt. This was all way out of pocket and I didn't know how it was going to end up. I mean shit, the Suicide Kings used a fucking bomb, tonight. They blew my place of work sky-fucking-high! I needed Aaron out of this. I needed him safe and I needed to make sure he stayed that way and so I did that, the only way I knew how. It was the biggest dick thing I could do or say, but I said it anyways:

"Sounds to me like you've made up your mind already," I said ,and licked my lips. I felt hot and shaky with adrenaline; I didn't want to do this, I didn't want to lose him, but I didn't want Aaron getting caught up in this mess.

"Andy, that's not what I meant, and you know it," he said, and his jaw set into stubborn lines.

"Isn't it? Dude, Aaron, it's cool. It was fun while it lasted, and MC life, it's not for everyone." I hung my head and palmed the back of my neck, so he couldn't see the tears welling in my eyes as I tried to say as nonchalantly as possible, "It –was– fun while it lasted, right?" I saw his shoulders drop and the stricken expression on his face through the edge of my vision and I felt like a grade-'A', number-one jackass.

"Andy..." His voice faltered.

"I'll get one of the girls to drive you home," I mumbled again, and I was out the door. I found Ash and Hayden, and Hayden slipped out to drive Aaron home while Ashton held me while I cried. Shit, this sucked. This sucked fucking hard.

12

D isney...

I got out of the back seat of Trig and Ash's red Jeep and was immediately assaulted by the acrid burning smell. The rest of the MC had stayed back at the clubhouse. It was just me, Trig, Ash and Rev. The shop had finally been cleared of investigators and we were here to listen to what the fire marshal and cops had to say.

It was mid-morning, drifting on towards afternoon, and the autumn sky was as bright and blue and cheery as could be. We'd met as a club to decide what to do, after Aaron had gone, and Doc had arrived, deciding that it was pretty much on like Donkey Kong with the Suicide Kings. They wanted to fuck with us, well, we weren't going to take it lying down. Almost all of the out-of-town Sacred Hearts Nomads and Chapter members who had answered Dragon and Dray's call had thrown their lot in with us. Our number of brothers swelled to where we were now more closely matched with the Suicide Kings and plans were under way to take them down a notch or two. For the time being though, those plans didn't include me, Trig, or Revelator. We had our livelihoods to rebuild, and from the looks of things they wouldn't be rebuilt here.

The shop looked like something out of the Gaza Strip, not like something smack-dab in the middle of Anytown, U.S.A. The front of the shop was just, gone… just blown out. Insulation was hanging like ribbons and charred timbers were jagged and threatening. I felt bad. The insurance company on one side of us and the sandwich shop on the other both had to close up shop, too. The building as a whole had to come down. Trig, Rev, and I waded through the wreckage to our respective work areas. There wasn't anything for Ashton to salvage from the front desk, the front desk was just gone. She picked her way carefully over the blackened streaks and chunks of cinderblock littering the black-and-white checkered floor and picked up one of the water-damaged framed news articles about Open Road off the scarred linoleum.

Tears sprang up in her golden eyes and she shook before breaking into a sob, and Trig was just there. His arms went around his woman and he pulled her such a loving and protective embrace that I felt the loss of Aaron like a knife in the gut. I pushed a filing cabinet out of my way and stepped into my alcove, which was, miraculously, mostly untouched. I opened my tool box and everything was in it, just fine. I picked up Rusty's tattoo gun and clutched it to my chest, and felt overcome with emotion myself.

The heavy-duty Husky tool box I used to store all my tattoo shit had protected it from the blast, and the fire hadn't reached over here. The tools of my trade were intact and the memories attached to them were, too. It was the only glimmer of hope to have come from this so far. I looked around me and at my brothers and friends, and felt just as blasted apart as the damned shop, but this wasn't the first time I'd had to tear down and build from the beginning. Hopefully it would be the last, though, because at the tender age of twenty-two, I was fucking tired of rebuilding from the ground up, only to have my shit knocked down and be forced to rebuild again.

"Hey, guys!" I heard Rev call out. "Thermo-fax is good!" I felt my shoulders slump in relief. That would have been a bitch to replace.

"My guns are cool, Disney, what about yours?" Trig called.

"All my shit's cool. Protected by the industrial tool-box you guys recommended," I called back.

"My guns are toast, but most of the piercing shit is good," Zander called.

We all met up out in the center of the shop floor, Ashton clinging to Trig.

"I'ma call Dray, have him get a U-Haul and bring it and some more guys. We need to get this shit out to the parking lot, before these guys say we can't be in here anymore." We made a plan, agreed to it and got our asses to work, which sucked hard for me with how much I hurt, but at the same time, was fucking perfect. It kept my mind off Aaron.

Dray had shown up with a U-Haul box truck with a pile of the nomads and outlying chapter guys, all looking at patching over into our chapter, trailing behind it.

Everett, who'd been driving the truck, was standing nearby with her best friend Mandy, they were comforting Ashton and helping her to box up what papers they could out of the shop's dented and water-logged filing cabinets.

When we'd gotten to the shop, my first priority had been to salvage as much of my livelihood as I could. My second priority was laying on her side dented to hell and back, and left me wondering if she would even start. I couldn't hoist her upright in my current state, so one of the FNG's (Fucking New Guys) did it for me.

"Man, it's a damn shame. You had her lookin' brand spankin' new. Saw her one of my first nights here, and been meaning to ask you about her." I looked at the guy. His strawberry blonde hair was shaved so close to his head you could see scalp, and he was built, the shoulders of his leather jacket and the cut overlaying them straining.

"What's your name?" I asked. I'm sure he'd told me but fuck if I could remember. He smiled and held out his hand.

"Red-Thirteen," he said. I raised an eyebrow.

"Disney," I took his hand and his shake was firm, "That's going to get confusing as fuck. Revelator calls her Red." I said, indicating

Mandy, who was carefully and efficiently sorting papers according to what Ashton was telling her.

"Naw, just call me Thirteen or R.T., it's not my first rodeo being around other 'Reds'," he said.

"No disrespect, but how the hell did you come by such a long road name?" I asked as we inspected the damage to Devi. I'd decided to keep the name Aaron had given her.

"Kind of embarrassing actually–" he started, but didn't get to finish. Dragon came over with another new guy.

"Thirteen, borrow you?" Dragon asked.

"Yeah, what's up, P.?" They wandered a distance away, heads together, and another new guy, who introduced himself quietly as Blue, helped Rev walk my thrashed bike up into the back of the old pick-up Dragon had rolled up in. I heaved a sigh. I had no idea how I was going to pay rent, let alone how I was going to fix my bike. Hell, my car was dead in a parking stall back at my apartment.

"Fuck," I swore low and hard.

"What's the matter, Puddin'?" Zander asked.

"Let's see, I'm out of a job, out of a car, out of a bike, out of a – boyfriend–, and now that I'm out of a job, I'm going to be out of a place to live, because I can't make my fucking rent on what I've made so far this month." I pushed my hands through my hair, the cast on my left wrist hard against my scalp and held the back of my head, fingers laced. I straightened up tall and let out an explosive breath. Revelator looked at me, his dark eyes sorrowful.

"Didn't know about Aaron, I'm sorry, man." He looked down at his red Converse high-tops and back up, "We'll find another place to set up shop. Can't do anything about the job until then but you had family in me and Trig before any of this shit went down. You got much shit to move?" I blinked.

"Just my tool box and bike, both are loaded I think," I said.

"No, dipshit, from your apartment," Rev said, exasperated.

"What are you getting at?" I asked.

"I got an empty room at the house you can have. Your apartment is a piece of shit and not worth the money you been dumping into living in it. We got the truck, let's dump the shop stuff off in my garage and go get your shit while we got it. Get it all done at once, Brother." He held out his hand and I blinked in confusion.

"You want my faggot ass to move in with you?" I asked, incredulous.

"One, don't ever call yourself that again," he said sharply. "Two, you got a better idea? I know you been living paycheck to paycheck. My place is straight-up mine. It doesn't look like much, but Hell, been in it by myself since my granddaddy died and left it to me; having a roommate might not be such a bad thing." I blinked stupidly for a second.

"You want me to move in with you?" I repeated, skeptically.

"Dude, Squick." I flinched at the old nickname; I didn't want to be that guy anymore. Revelator pushed on, "Tattooing is all you got, it's what you do, it's fucking what you're good at, fuck, you're one of the best I've ever seen. Me, I got tattooing and piercing, sure but I can make more off one fight than I can spending an entire month sticking people with needles!" He looked at me and I nodded slowly. Everything was this total nightmare whirlwind and I felt like I had yet to fucking land, but I already knew I wasn't in fucking Kansas anymore.

"Okay," I said, because what other choice did I have? I didn't have enough money for rent and rent was due in two weeks. I wasn't going to find a new job, or open a new shop with these guys, or make enough money doing either inside two weeks, so why fucking fight it?

"Okay?" he asked.

"Okay," I affirmed.

Okay.

13

———

Disney...

  I'd spent the last three days with Ashton in Rev's garage sorting through the shit we'd salvaged from the shop. We were getting nowhere with the paperwork. Zander was training in his home gym, to get back into fighting for the time being and Trig, well, Trig could do work from home under the table, even though he didn't have to. Ashton more than had them covered. Shelly's genius with numbers had seen the money she'd gotten from her douchebag ex-husband's death grow rather than shrink, even with dropping a huge chunk of change into Ev and Mandy's shop and the clubhouse renovations.

We were worried about Ev and Mandy's shop, even though everything had gone through Ashton, and the club was nowhere near it. The club hadn't had a whole lot to do with Open Road Ink, either; they'd just provided startup funds in the tattoo shop's beginning when the club had been looking for legitimate ventures to go into after Dragon's Old Lady had been killed. Open Road Ink had been one of those ventures, Open Road Garage had been another.

Now I was sitting on the edge of my new bed in my new room at Zander's with my cellphone in my hands, watching the cursor on the white screen blink off and on, my thumbs poised over the touch-screen keyboard. I missed Aaron. I wanted so badly to see if this was something we could talk about, something we could fix or deal with... or try to anyways.

I hadn't heard anything from him since we parted ways at the club, and that sucked. Hard. I'd been staring at my phone for the last fifteen minutes, keeping the screen from going dark, trying to think of what the Hell to say, when it buzzed in my hands. It was a text message from Aaron.

Aaron: I don't want it to end like this. Please. Meet me?

My breath caught in my lungs and my thumbs twitched... I waited a heartbeat, then two, then cautiously tapped out a response. It was awkward holding the phone with the black cast on my wrist.

Okay. Where?

I held my breath and scraped my lower lip through my teeth while I anxiously waited for a reply. The sound of my lip ring clicking against my teeth was offset by the clanking weights from Rev's home gym.

Aaron: My place?

I wanted that but at the same time, I didn't know if that was such a good idea. I pursed my lips. I couldn't think of anyplace else more neutral. I couldn't and wouldn't do it here after just moving in, and I wouldn't take it to the clubhouse either, so I gave in.

Fine. I need to find a ride. You going anywhere?

The message came back immediately.

Aaron: No. I'll be waiting.

"Zander!" I called out and heard his bellow from his home gym.

"What?"

"Borrow your car?"

"Yeah! Keys are on the hook inside the front door! You scratch her, I beat you! Got it?" he called back.

"Got it!" I affirmed, and heard weights clang to the floor.

I pulled on some fresh clothes and was just straightening from pulling on my boots when his compact frame filled the doorway, his shoulders nearly touching the doorjamb to either side of him.

"Going to see Aaron?" he asked.

"Yeah," I said, shrugging into my jacket and cut.

"Good luck, man. I mean it about the car." He turned to the side so I could go out past him.

"I know, thanks." I went out to the living room and retrieved the keys to his Chevelle off the hook and slipped out into the rain. I took off my cut and folded it neatly over my arm before getting into the car. The rain pattered softly on the roof, the inside windows fogging around the edges. I started the 68 Chevelle SS and it roared to life. Zander had put a lot of love, time, and care into restoring her. She was a beautiful cherry-red with white racing stripes and I was suddenly nervous about taking her out of the driveway, but I did it anyway.

The drive to Aaron's felt like a long one, my heart throbbing painfully in my chest, my cheeks hot as I filled from the bottom to the top with a soul-crushing anxiety about how things were going to unfold. I pulled into a free parking space next to Aaron's Subaru and cut the engine. I wanted to get back to work, somehow, somewhere, and build myself my bike. My Mazda sat at Open Road Garage and would be fixed and sold. I didn't mind riding in all weather for the time being, if it meant I had another project that would net me something like this car at its end.

I sat for a long time, frozen in my seat, hands sliding back and forth over the black steering wheel. Out to the sides and back in, out to the sides and back in. I didn't know what it was about Aaron that tied me in freaking knots so hard after barely knowing him. I couldn't explain it, I didn't think it really needed explaining. Just something about being near him soothed my soul. When I was in his presence everything felt right, and natural, and, I don't know... I just felt like, when I was with him or near him, that I was the kind of me that I always wanted to be.

I took a deep breath and let it out slow, and reached for the door handle. I got out of the car, pulling my cut from the passenger seat with me and I stared down at the singed patches on its back for a moment, before shrugging it on. I locked the car and took the steps to the second floor two at a time. About four doors down from Aaron's, I heard it, and it slowed my pace. Music, but not just any kind of music, the mournful tones of a cello drifted down the open aired corridor to reach me.

I'd never heard him play, at least not until now. It made me feel incredibly sad to realize that this was how it was, the first time I got to hear it could be the very last time I ever got to. I stepped carefully up the hall and rested my forehead against his front door and listened for a time. The way he played was flawless, perfect and deliberate and just so rich and beautiful, like the man himself. The piece was incredibly sad and I felt a little guilty that I didn't have a freaking clue what it was. I mean, music was so much a part of Aaron's life. The man he was with should be interested in what his boyfriend played, shouldn't he?

I vowed right then and there that if we somehow made it through the next few minutes into something resembling a relationship, that I would learn the difference between classical composers. I mean I loved music and musicals, but was a little lost on the difference between Beethoven and Chopin and the lot.

I took a deep breath to steady myself and still my racing thoughts and raised my hand to knock. The sound my knuckles made against the door was sharp and loud, and immediately the beautiful music stopped. I took a step-and-a-half back, so Aaron could see me through the peephole. It darkened, then lightened, and I could hear him throwing back the bolt and chain and then, suddenly, he was there, beautiful and lean, the deep dark wells of his eyes blinking beneath that dyed shock of fiery hair and I ached to reach out and pull him to me. To kiss him, to touch and hold him, but I did none of those things. Instead, I thrust my hands into my jeans pockets and pursed my lips and waited to see what he would do.

I didn't want to open myself up to any more hurt than I was already feeling, but that was a lot harder than it sounded with him standing there in his worn white tee and comfortable butter-soft jeans. He was barefoot and scrumptious, and the pain in my chest was worsening by the second as I fought my feelings down and tried valiantly to thrust them into a box, lock it up and toss the key. It'd only been three days and I fucking missed him like it'd been months.

"Hi," he said softly, and pushed his glasses up higher on his nose.

"Hi," I grunted back. He held the door wider and stretched, his shirt lifting to give me a peek at the flat expanse of his stomach, and I closed my eyes and dropped my head, fixing my gaze resolutely onto the carpet. I brushed past him and his hand shot out and closed around the arm of my jacket. I froze.

"Andy, I'm so sorry," he said and I nodded, mutely. I was sorry, too. Sorry that I couldn't just change. That good, bad, or indifferent, I was committed to the club and my brothers in it and sometimes that came with some real ugly and heavy shit, like the Suicide Kings.

"Please, talk to me?" he asked softly, and closed the door behind us.

"I'm a little torn in two, I guess," I said, my throat tightening. He drew me along with him and we sat on the end of his bed, which really was the only place to sit.

"Talk to me," he implored.

"I like you, Aaron. As impossible and scary and just as damned fast as it is, I might even love you a little, but at the same time, I'm committed to and love every single person in my club and I won't leave. I can't leave." I forced my eyes to his which were full of compassion and something else I couldn't quite define. He picked up my hands in his.

I pressed on, "I don't want anything to happen to you, Aaron. I want so much to be with you, but I can't and won't leave them to do it, and if letting you be is what it takes to keep you safe, then, I will but I really, really don't want to." Damn it. I was going to cry. I felt the tears well up hot and immediate and I just didn't have it in me to be the strong one this time, because I really wanted this. I really wanted a shot at having a partner-in-crime, someone to share laughs and love and just everything that my boss and friend Trigger had with Ashton and my mentor Reaver had with his wife Hayden. At the same time, I had no right to drag him in to such a potentially volatile and violent situation.

Aaron pulled me into him and held me, making soothing noises. He pulled back to search my face and pressed his lips to mine and my misery was complete, because to me, the kiss tasted like good-bye. I rested my forehead against his, savoring the moment, if it were to be my last, when he surprised me.

"I don't want that, either. I want to try. What happened scared the piss out of me; I thought you were dead, I thought I was going to get there and that you were going to be gone before I ever really had the chance..." he choked up, took a deep breath, held it and let it out and said, "I'm willing to risk it if you are."

Our mouths crashed together, I couldn't be sure if it was me that kissed him or him that kissed me, and it suddenly wasn't at all important. What was important was that finally, someone was willing to take a chance on me. The real me. The unmasked and vulnerable me, the whole package, and not just the parts that suited them. First my club, and now this man, this beautiful, beautiful man.

We made love, and with every kiss and touch and lick I silently vowed to Aaron that I would do everything in my power to keep him safe from the mess the club was in. To keep everyone safe that I could. Since the Lake, it had sort of become the unspoken rule that I was the defender of the women, the last line of defense should shit get real and I was okay with that. I was more than okay with that, because the girls mattered to me. Aaron mattered to me and for all intents and purposes he was considered one of the girls by club standards.

We stayed in and woke to the shrill ring of my phone the next morning. I answered it on the fourth ring.

"Yeah?" I groused into the phone.

"Hey, Puddin', you work things out with yer man?" Rev asked, and I smiled as Aaron's dark eyes met mine, an answering smile sparkling in their depths.

"Yeah," I answered, "I think we're straight." Aaron kissed my chest and I felt a contented sigh escape me.

"Good, then can you bring back my fucking car?" I barked a laugh and Aaron laughed too, having heard Rev loud and clear.

"Can I get some breakfast?" I asked.

"No," was the short answer and he hung up. Okay, he had a right to be irritated, I guess. That didn't stop me from spending long minutes kissing

AARON or from taking an extra-long shower with him, though.

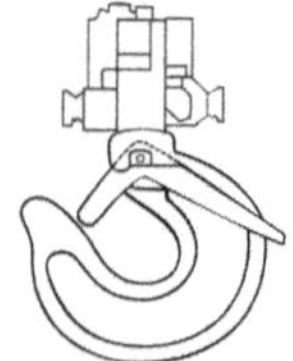

Ghost...

"You're sure, man?"

I fixed my eyes on the boxy cartoon rendition of Satan, complete with ram's horns and back dropped with cartoon flames on the side of Disney's neck.

"I'm sure," I affirmed.

This was my first tattoo and a pretty big step. I hadn't been patched in more than a few months but I'd been a part of this club for almost a year and a half. It was time to ink the devotion I felt towards these guys under my skin and I wanted Disney to be the one to do it.

"You sure you don't want Trig to do this?" he asked, working the latex gloves between his long fingers, finding a comfortable fit.

"I'm sure, man," I said and smiled. While it was true Trig was, and always would be my brother-in-arms, the guy who took a bullet for me and who saved my ass countless times over there, I wanted Disney to know that I knew he had my back. Rev wasn't half so insecure and when the topic of club ink had come up, I'd known right away I'd wanted it to be Disney that did mine.

"I don't get it." The kid frowned and I smiled.

"Just stop being a pussy and get to it,, already!" I teased, which just made him frown harder.

"We'll see who the pussy is in a minute," he griped and smeared some Vaseline onto the swell of the outside of my left shoulder.

"Ha, ha," I said and took a pull off my beer. We were at Trigger and Ashton's in Trigger's small 'studio' just off the living room. The room was really just big enough for his tool box of ink and needles, a massage chair, his little rolling doctor's stool, and the little metal table where he laid out all of his stuff. He had an autoclave low to the ground on a squat little table wedged up under where the ceiling sloped because of the stairs.

We could hear Trigger, Ashton, and Disney's boyfriend Aaron all talking in the living room. It was still taking some getting used to, Disney being out of the closet and all, and for the most part it was all right, but I still caught myself cringing inwardly whenever the two men held hands or kissed, which was bullshit on my part. Old habits died hard though, I guess, I mean I was raised in the Midwest around people who liked to picket soldiers' funerals with signs proclaiming 'God Hates Fags', which was an even bigger pile of bullshit.

It took joining the Corps and finding out one of our unit was gay after they repealed Don't Ask/Don't Tell for me to realize that gay, straight, or a little crooked, none of it fucking mattered. Jack was a cool dude before I knew he was gay and he was a cool dude after, just like Disney who was peeling the tracing paper stencil off my arm. I cocked my elbow out from my body and looked down at the blue lines on my arm etching out the emblem of the Sacred Hearts MC.

Unlike most of the guy's renditions done in blacks and whites, mine would be full color. I'd lived my life in blacks and whites for long enough. It took meeting Trig, and a couple of tours in the bland, drab desserts of Afghanistan to really appreciate that things weren't always black-and-white, good and bad, on one side of the line or the other with no in-between. I vowed never to live that way again if I could avoid it.

"You ready?" Disney asked.

"Ask you a question first?"

He looked at me and used the back of his brightly-colored arm to push some of his lank brown hair out of his eyes.

"Yes, I think you're pretty, but no, you aren't my type. Aaron is my type." he said automatically and I blinked before scoffing.

"Damn right, I'm pretty, but that wasn't what I was gonna ask, smart-ass," I said and he gave me a devil-may-care grin. I tried not to shift uncomfortably. Being told by a dude I was pretty was fucking weird, but the sparkle in Disney's eye straight-up told me he was yanking my fucking chain.

"Shoot. What's your question?" he asked.

"Shelly talk to you? You know... about what happened?" I asked, quietly, afraid to be overheard. Disney heaved a sigh and shook his head, and I think his heart was just as heavy as mine.

"No, man. Not a word. I know she had to move in with Reaver and Hayden, though. They're supposed to be moving her stuff this weekend into storage, she's gonna live in their spare room," he said, his voice low.

"Why, what happened?" I asked, worried.

"Stopped getting up, stopped going to work, stopped paying her bills, she just stopped everything." He sighed heavily and gave a one-shouldered shrug as he twisted this and that on his tattoo gun. It was a sentiment that I echoed, except I was drowning in guilt over what had happened to her. If only I'd been less of a stubborn ass and talked with her, reasoned with her like a grown-up rather than just standing around with my thumb up my ass, hoping she was some kind of Goddamned mind-reader. I scrubbed my face with my hands and took another irritated pull off my beer.

"Can I offer a piece of unsolicited advice?" Disney asked softly.

"Yeah, man, whatcha got?" I asked, just as quietly.

"Be what Shelly needs, not what she wants. You had it right the first time and what happened to her, it wasn't her fault, but it wasn't yours, either. It was that asshole's fault and we may not have been able to stop it from happening to Shells, but we definitely stopped it from happening to anyone else's cousin, sister, daughter, niece... you get me?" His brown eyes were serious as he looked me over and I found myself nodding slowly. I felt slightly less guilty, but by no means was I completely absolved of it. Only two people could do that for me, and one wasn't speaking to me. Me, well, it would be a while before I could forgive myself. I was working on it, though. Some nights were better than others on that front.

"And, brother," Disney said breaking me out of my reverie.

"Yeah?" I asked.

"This," he said, plucking my beer out of my hand and rolling over to the toolbox, "isn't helping you or her." He set the bottle resolutely out of my reach and rolled back across the polished cement floor.

I gave him a half-assed mock salute but found myself nodding, chagrined. After all, it was Disney that had cleaned up after my last drunken escapade. It wasn't something I did often, but I felt bad about it, just the same.

"So that's it, huh?" I asked as he smeared some goop on my arm and poised the gun to start. "Be what she needs, and not what she wants."

"That's the best I can figure," he said somberly. "Shelly needs someone to look out for her. Reaver has his hands full with Hayden and starting the next round of his life, and truth be told, he's been looking out for Shells since they were kids. Not sure what's going on there. But she goes on these wild self-destructive benders. Just never anything this bad before. Even Reaver's knocked a little sideways with how bad it's been." The buzz of the tattoo gun was sharp in the small space as I let his words sink in. I barely felt the sting as he laid in the very first line of my very first tattoo, lost down the rabbit-hole of my own thoughts as I was.

"Something happen to her? Before Sparks, I mean?" I mused aloud.

I wasn't really asking Dis, but he answered me anyways by shrugging and saying, "Who can say?"

Only one or two people that I knew of, and I wasn't going to ask Reaver. I thought about it as I fell into an almost meditative state between the buzz of the tattoo gun and the endorphins that began to kick in after a couple of minutes of minor discomfort.

Be what Shelly needed. Not what she wanted. Hadn't that been what I was trying to do in the first place? I sat still while Disney mercilessly ground ink into my arm with a look that was a cross between sheer concentration and apologetic sympathy, which, the hell if I knew how he pulled that off, just as I had no notion of how the fuck I was going to be what Shelly needed at a time like this in her life.

There was only one thing I knew for sure, and it was a lesson I learned well behind the scope. I needed to wait, to be patient, for an opportunity to present itself. Once it did, I needed to jump on it. I needed to not hesitate for anything, and to pull the damned trigger.

Yeah. That's what I needed to do. I needed to wait and be ready, and from the sound of things, I wouldn't have to wait too long. At least I hoped that was the case.

Not just for my sake, but for the sake of my ice princess with the sapphire eyes.

ALSO BY A.J. DOWNEY

ABOUT THE AUTHOR

A.J. Downey is the internationally bestselling author of The Sacred Hearts Motorcycle Club romance series. She is a born and raised Seattle, WA Native. She finds inspiration from her surroundings, through the people she meets, and likely as a byproduct of way too much caffeine.

She has lived many places and done many things, though mostly through her own imagination...An avid reader all of her life, it's now her turn to try and give back a little, entertaining as she has been entertained.

Stalker Information:
www.ajdowney.com